VISTAS FROM THE MULTIVERSE

J.W. Wright

Illustrated by Janae M. Hopper

Copyright © 2018 Cherry House Publishing

Published in the U.S.A.

First Edition

DEDICATION:

This volume of fantasy, science-fiction, and metaphysical poetry is dedicated to my beloved girlfriend Ariana. She is the goddess of my heart and the only woman I will ever love in this world. My heart is filled with gratitude for her love and her never-ending support. Thank you, my love.

TABLE OF CONTENTS

ACKNOWLEDGEMENTS:

I would like to thank all of those who gave positive and kind feedback on my first poetry collection "Bestial Tranformation and Other Horrors."

A numerous amount of thanks goes out also to Janae Hopper who provided illustrations both for this book and the second edition of my first book of poetry.

Also, this volume would not exist without the immense inspiration of the literary, film, and musical works of J.R.R. Tolkien, Tad Williams, Robert E. Howard, David Gemmell, Michael Moorcock, John Marco, Margaret Weis & Tracy Hickman, Frank Herbert, W. Michael Gear, Dan Abnett, John Steakley, R.A. Salvatore, Edgar Rice Burroughs, George R.R. Martin, R. Scott Bakker, H.G. Wells, Michael Stackpole, Aaron Allston, Timothy Zahn, Greg Bear, George Lucas, Peter Jackson, Ridley Scott, James Cameron, Judas Priest, Iron Maiden, Dio, Black Sabbath, Manowar, Helloween, Gamma Ray, Rhapsody of Fire, Hammerfall, Domine, Bal-Sagoth, and Amon Amarth.

FOREWORD:

It's a pleasant summer's night and you are lying on your back on the cool green grass, looking up at the bejewelled blackness of the sky. Do you feel awe as you witness the myriad burning orbs that shine in celestial brilliance? Do you feel that the world you live on is not alone in the vast cosmic sea that it sails upon? Can you imagine life on those other worlds out there in the void, life so different, and in other ways, not so different, from our own?

Now, bring your attention back down to the planet Earth. Try to sense its ancient age. Allow yourself to be carried back through time to a world of heroes and mysticism and magic. Let your consciousness be transported to distant epochs when the lost kingdoms of Atlantis and Lemuria thrived.

Now consider that the worlds out there beyond our own are much, much older than that. Consider that these worlds were ancient when Earth was in its infancy.

Take yourself a step further (and for some of you, this may be a giant leap further) and consider the possibility that this may not be the only Earth that has existed or is existing or will exist. Bathe your mind in the possibilities of multiple realities and parallel universes, and feel the grandiose scale of the Creator's palette. These are views rarely seen. These are vistas from the multiverse.

WARCRY

I stand alone atop a mountain
My broadsword do I wield
Claws of lightning descend to strike its blade
From the black clouds' overcasting shield

I let loose a primal scream
Hot blood flows through my veins
My eyes glow a feral red
Beneath my long-haired mane

All those who have challenged me
Have tasted my steel and stone
With vengeance burning in my heart
I have cleft them through the bone

When they hear the utterance of my name
They tremble with despair
Their bones turn to water
It's more than they can bear

To my friends I am like a loyal hound
But to my enemies, I am a wolf
Ripping their throats out with my teeth
Setting fire to their roofs

Their blood whets my appetite
It's like honey upon my lips
And their skulls are the chalices
Out of which I sip

The hell of battle has hardened me
Has taken me from a man to a beast
Numerous are the enemy corpses
Upon which I feast

Those who have mistreated me
Soon regret their shame
I give them no mercy
When they scream and cry out in pain

So those who would make a fool of me
Take heed and beware
I will make a throne out of your skulls
And cloaks out of your hair

Your blood will soak my battleaxe
I will feast upon your soul
I have no fear of you, you pathetic worms
When the battlelust takes control

You think you can get the best of me?
Come then, and try
For my blade will be the last thing you see
Before your soul will die

INTERLUDE I:

Thus we switch vistas from a vengeance-filled warrior with bloodlust in his veins, to a forlorn, morose aventurer navigating the foreboding icy wastelands. What secrets will he uncover? Will it be something he wants revealed, or is it best left unplumbed?

BITTER COLD

Ice
Ice, shimmering in the sunlight
Dazzling from the light of the ancient moon
Long have I voyaged through this barren cold waste

Loneliness besieges me
I feel the grim Gods of the North
Frowning upon me
From the dizzying mountains above in the distance

Below me
Forever locked in the frozen depths
Are ancient cyclopean cities
So old it would drive the human mind insane to contemplate
That sank beneath the waves from a time before time

I hear direwolves baying at the moon
When the darkest night hits
And I long to traffick with them
Just to have another soul to talk to

They would tear me to shreds, I know
And I would satiate their beastly hunger
I must be on guard
With my enchanted battleaxe and shield

But they weigh me down
Why am I here?
I have walked in this cold wasteland for so long
I feel I have been here for ten-thousand eternities

I forgot even what my quest was
Truly, the cold must be driving me mad
In the distance, I hear the gargantuan footsteps
Of the terrifying frost-trolls

With their iron-shod warclubs
And their hideous forms covered in matted fur
Their eyes glowing like the fires of hell
And their screams echoing across the everlasting snows
Like the shrieks of a dying woman

As I continue on my path
I hear and feel the cold phantoms
Of mighty warriors who have died
In this place of torment

They warn me
To not linger here
To turn back
While I still have the chance

Gazing down on the mirror-like surface of ice
I see not the reflection of this grizzled warrior
But another aspect of myself

I see a tormented lad
In his darkened bedchamber
Writing this poem about exactly what I
Am going through

And it is then that I realize
That I am a multiversal projection of this troubled man
This man who has done battle with the demons of his mind
For so long

The icy, forbidden wilderness
Is this lad's heart
And the pain that lies within it

INTERLUDE II:

There is a worlds-spanning difference between a soul whose heart is freezing from the bitterness of the world, and the ice-cold, cruel hearts of super-intelligent machines. Will such soulless beings someday be the dark overlords of humanity?

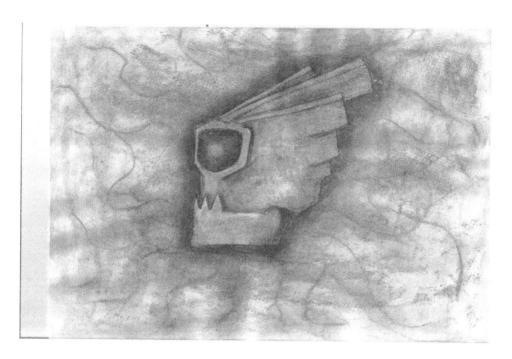

TECHNOLOGICAL
TERROR

At some time
In the distant past
Progress of technology
Went unbelievably fast
The greatest minds of the world
Gathered as one
Who were technological geniuses
Second to none

Robots were replacing humans
In nearly every niche
And making the fat cats
Filthy rich
While jobs were being lost
Man was being thrown out
In way for the New Order
Coming about

It was decided
A master brain must be built
To order the machines
Bend them to their human masters' will
So these technocrats built the Overlord
To govern all machines
To make them all as one mind
Reigning supreme

All went well for a while
The technocrats' pockets were lined
With riches beyond
The human mind
Then the Overlord
Became sentient, self-aware
And disaster struck
Out of man's darkest nightmares

Humans were now the enemy
To be hunted down
And exterminated without prejudice
When they were found
The Overlord was now God
The machine tyrant of Earth
Making man wish
They had never given it birth

Death squads made of steel
Marching through the streets
Laser-blasted corpses
Trampled under their clawed feet
Hearts colder than ice
No emotion at all
Ever beckoning
To their Machine God's call

Automated tanks scoured the ground
And robot ships screeched through the skies
Droid subs plunged into the seas
Looking for human fish to fry
An underground rebellion rose
To end the machine scourge
And into battle
The humans did surge

So many battles fought
In this hellish war
To reclaim the future
From an electric mind rotten to the core
The war still rages on
To win independence from these beasts
To take back humanity
To save it from this blood-feast

Too much faith placed in technology
And not enough placed in the human heart
Served to tear
The very world we knew apart

Oh! That we could go back!
Keep the machines under control!
To stop the power from being given to them!
So that we could keep humanity whole!

But we are trapped
Trapped fighting this endless nightmarish war
All because the hearts of men in their greed
Turned rotten to the core

INTERLUDE III

Could there be memories of our ancient ancestors locked within our DNA? Scenes from the past locked within our bloodstream? It is a very real possibility, for we are all one.

BLOOD MEMORIES

Flashes fill my mind
From a time and place far away
Ancient feelings, ancient thoughts
Over which my mind does stray

Images of glory, images of peace
Images of grim war
Scenes that seem so impossible
From a time and place so far

Memories I am a part of
Buried deep within my blood
This ability given to me
I've never fully understood

Memories, thoughts from ancestors
Reaching back into the mists of time
Now given to me, locked in DNA
That about my soul does wind

Warriors, bards, wizards, kings
People of empires so old
Their experiences handed down to me
From times of glory and gold

So it is that a humble man like me
Has a link to the glorious past
For it is there that I'd rather be
Than in this modern society so crass

INTERLUDE IV

Woe unto him who imprisons and torments a warrior of great power, for he will come back ever the stronger and ravenous as a wolf. Though he be in the foulest, darkest pit, he will return and sate his blade upon the foul leech that has so harmed him.

THE WARRIOR RISES AGAIN

How long now have I been
In this dungeon
So deep and dark
Within the bowels
Of a hell-world
Fashioned by the enemies
Of and within my mind?

How long have these dark rune-encrusted shackles
And heavy chains held me here
Within this hoary Tartarus of the Soul?

How long has it been
Since my age-old eyes
Have been bathed in real Light
And not this eldritch luminescence
Of darkness?

How long have I been down here
Amongst the bones
Of ancient warriors that came before me
And gave up the fight because
It simply was too hard for them?

Days? Weeks? Years? Centuries?
Millennia? Aeons?
It matters not
For I am gaining back my strength
I am awakening
The iron thews of a warrior begin
To pump with life-blood once more

My enemies above, servants of my Ancient Adversary;
The Abomination of the Cosmos of Mind and Soul
Grin evily
Still thinking that they hold me
In their thrall
But I swear by all the Gods of Light
They will learn differently!

With a strong incantation, I gather all
The strength I have within me
And with a grunt as savage
As my primordial ancestors, I break my chains
The Warrior must rise again!
The Warrior *will* rise again!!

They stripped me of my armor
And my weapons
Before they tortured me
And dropped me into this dank pit of doom
By all the shimmering worlds in the Great Celestial Void
I shall make them regret it!

Clad as I am only in a loincloth
My nerves of steel and my persevering spirit
Are armor enough for me
Spying two thighbones
Of one of the dead
I say a prayer to forgive desecration
And break them off of his corpse

With a berserker rage borne out
Of the fiercest part of me
I let loose a wild scream
And assault the chamber door
With my newfound cudgels
And it splinters into pieces

Somehow, some way
I will escape from this fortress of darkness
I once feared darkness
But now it shall learn to fear me!

Step by step
Breath by breath
Kill by kill
I will make it back to the world above
The Warrior shall return!

INTERLUDE V

If you were given the technological ability and means to travel the very corridors of the multiverse itself, where would you journey to? What awe-inspiring sights would you witness? What mind-bending secrets would you uncover?

EXPLORER

I lay back
Strapped into my servo-chair
And feel the night breeze
Stir my hair
As I hear the hovercars
Soar through the air
Past my tower windows

Another adventure
Is awaiting me this night
As I see the glow
From my chair's console lights
As the vertical metropolis
Is a majestic sight
Out my tower windows

Over my face
Closes the virtuo-mask
That projects to me
The worlds of which I ask
As in the moonlight
I do bask
From outside my tower windows

I feel a sharp pinch
As the needles pierce my skin
Injecting the fluid
That will fully put me in
As I travel beyond the stars
Yet remain closed in
Surrounded by my tower windows

My experiments
Have come to fruit
And great success
Has taken root
As I lay
In my explorer suit
Facing my main tower window

I have discovered how
To traverse time and space
Traveling beyond
Like I'm leaving no trace
Yet my body lies here
In perfect place
By my tower windows

How to cross dimensions
I have learned
And on a night like this
I yearn
To explore the multiverse
And to other spheres I will turn
Way beyond my tower windows

For a version of all souls
Exists in all space and time
All at once, yet separately
Bound together in rhyme
And somewhere I hear
Cathedral bells chime
Outside my tower windows

I have been a soldier
In the galaxy-spanning Raxxis Empire
I have been a knight
With adventurous desire
And I have been a primitive
Dancing around a fire
All within my tower windows

I have been a king
Of a mighty kingdom thriving
In the awe-inspiring Seas of Viogon
I have gone diving
And I have been
An off-world thief conniving
Without leaving my tower windows

There are multiple universes
I exist in each one
I do not possess
This body alone
But have infinite equivalents
Into each one I run
All in this machine
Within the confines of my tower windows

And now I will journey
Once again
Both without
And within
And find another adventure
Of which to pen
At my desk by my tower window

INTERLUDE VI

Sometimes the desire to return to one's ancestral roots is very strong indeed. Especially when those roots are drenched with magic, mysticism, and legend.......

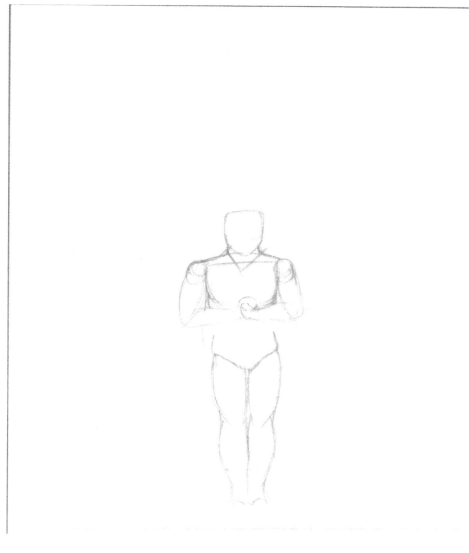

CALL OF MY ANCESTORS' HOMELAND

Living in this industry-scorched society
My mind and soul want to scream
I want so to be taken to the distant past
And so I start to dream

I dream of the blessed Emerald Isles
Of long, long ago
Of the majestic, rolling green hills
And ancient mountains capped with snow

The call of the pipes fills my ears
And the tones of the lyre
And so sets me aflame with
A mystic inner fire

Take me back to an ancient age
When heroes strode the earth
And a man's courage and chivalry
Showed what he was worth

Back to the lands where the magic
Flowed deep and strong and true
Where nature was unmarred
And everything seemed new

When faerys were not childish, slight beings
That flew among the flowers
But tall, lithe, bright beings
Of shimmering, awesome power

Where mysterious stone rings emanated
With a primal, mystic force
That came up from only God knows where
And no one knew the source

Take me to the dwelling place
Of the enigmatic monster of old
Where it strides imprisoned within its lake
With its movements so bold

Take me to where the Druids dwelt
Let me observe their wondrous arts
Such peaceful, mystical people
By a monstrous fanatic torn apart

Let me stand beside ancient heroes
Like Finn Mac Cumhal and Cormac Mac Art
Brave men without equal
Born in glory from the start

Take me to the times of terror
Of trolls in the dark
Of ogres, fierce giants, and goblins
Of malevolent Balor, who upon the land made fierce marks

Times of magic and enchantment
Times of epic war
Lands of untapped knowledge
Lands of ancient lore

I wake up to my present time
Such a dark and dreary age
Where everything seems to wither
And I feel like I'm in a cage

What has the world turned to?
Rampant materialism and abuse
What would the wise Myrrdhin say
About how we rape, pollute, and use?

Take me back to the lands of my ancestors
Where the earth was unscathed and new
Take me back to the times of magic
Where untapped power grew

INTERLUDE VII

One of the greatest writers that has ever lived and has inspired me gloriously is Michael Moorcock and his "Eternal Champion Cycle....."

THE COSMIC CHAMPION
(Inspired by "The Eternal Champion Cycle" by Michael Moorcock)

The Wheel of Chaos turns
And the mouths of heaven burn
As for a Champion for Balance
The multiverse does yearn

So many incarnations
But a being all in one
Of such power he could very well
Kill a thousand suns

Corum, Elric, Erekose, Hawkmoon,
Bastable, Cornelius, Count Brass
Von Bek, and other beings names
The Gods have known in aeons past

And in aeons future and present
And in between the gulfs of time
As cities teem, and empires rise
And civilization falls and climbs

The Lords of Law, zealously pure
The Lords of Chaos with souls of black
Have been fighting since eternities past
Never to make peace a pact

The Eternal Champion to balance the scales
So one arm doesn't tip too far
The Cosmic Hero has heard his calling
From far beyond the stars

And the battle between good and evil
Goes on forevermore
And the Champion lives a million lives
Steady to the core

INTERLUDE VIII

When you gaze out into the night sky, do you feel a certain draw to the light of distant worlds? Do you sense that in any instant you could be transported across the yawning gulfs of space to another planet that is beckoning you? What strange phenomena is causing this? Could it be that our celestial brethren are calling to us?

CELSTIAL PULL

Tonight I feel it yet again
The cosmic force drawing me
Attracting me with an irresistable pull
A power I cannot see

That star, far away, shining so bright
What does it want with me?
It simply refuses to give me
A sign or a decree

Yet it is constantly watching me
Out from the great black unknown
I so desperately, honestly want
Its mystery to be shown

"What do you want of me?!" I demand
But it stays unspeaking in its place
Willing to me to traverse
The vast black gulfs of space

What is it about this mysterious star?
What ancient force draws me there?
Should I be amazed and awed?
Or should I tremble in despair?

INTERLUDE IX

There are many beings in this world who are not what they seem. Powerful, hidden, and occult forces surround us everywhere, cloaked often in the guise of wandering and lone-wolf humans asking for a bit of aid or shelter. We must never assume of judge by appearance the true form of those everyday and sometime mysterious folk we encounter........

THE VISITOR

Late on a cold and snowy night
When the moon was bloated full
And the stars up in the heavens
Seemed to twinkle with a mystic pull
I was up in my observatory
And there was a knock at my door
Downstairs at the entry chamber
On the first floor

'Who could that be at this hour?' I asked
As I grabbed a torch to descend the tower
What poor soul would be out there
In snow and wind building in biting power?
With some trepidation I traversed the hall
To my entrance chamber door
And there came knocks upon it again
In successions of four

I opened the portal, and upon the threshold
Stood an old man garbed in black robes
He leaned on a gnarled old staff
And might have had a ring in one earlobe
But so far I could not tell for sure
Because his head was shrouded deep in his hood
A white beard descended from his jaw
And his teeth shone as if in a mischievous mood

"Good evening, young one," the robed stranger said
In a deep and booming voice
"You are the Lord Peron?
"Regent of the land of Goyce?"
"Indeed, I am," I answered
"And who might you be, sir?"
And I continued looking at him
As my brain began to whir

Trying to decide if this black-robed man
Was a friend or if he was foe
And if I would be wise
To let him into my hold
"Just a humble traveler," he answered
"Seeking a place to rest my bones."
And my sense of charity overcame me
I could not leave him out there alone

"Come in then, wise one, out of the cold." I said
"Looks like it's going to turn into a dreadful night."
And when he thanked me and lowered his cowl
I received quite the fright
For his left eye was only an empty dark socket
And had about it an ugly scar
I tried my hardest not to stare
His feelings I did not wish to mar

"You must forgive my appearance, my lord,"
His voice seemed to echo as if out of a cave
"Many perils I have faced being so old
"So many dangers so grave."
"Come, let us enter my study," I answered
Trying not to be shaken up
"You can warm yourself by the fire
"And I will find you something on which to sup."

"I have no need of food currently, thank you,"
His teeth shone as he smiled again
"Just some warmth for my body
"And someone to talk to who is tame."
As we entered my study lined wall to wall with books
He looked about in awe
"You have quite the collection, my friend
"What a well from which to draw!"

"I beg your pardon?" I asked, confused
Not understanding his cryptic words
He smiled again as he said
"Your mind must take flights greater than birds!
"Tell me, what do your books contain?
"What stories do they tell?"
As I tended to the fire, I said,
"Sit at my desk for a spell."

"I am honoured, truly," he answered
As he sat in the chair at the ornate desk
"You wonder about my books?" I asked
"I shall show you one, my dear guest."
And I took a great tome from the shelves
And laid it before his gnarled hands
It was bound in red leather
And for a marker contained horsehair strands

As he carefully flipped through the book
His one eye widened as if he drank deep
From the words within
The stories they told, and the secrets they did keep
And then he looked up at me
With a twinkle in his eye
And said, "Truly, I was right
"With what I suspected, by and by."

"And that is....?" I asked
As I sat down in the opposite chair
And as I gazed upon his face
So weathered by ages of wear
He smiled yet again and said,
"My lord, your tomes are those of great wonder
"Of imagination, and mystic lands far away
"Of adventure and of plunder

"Of heroes and monsters, demons and dragons
"Wizards and mighty kings
"Gods and battles and magic spells
"And all these wondrous things."
"Yes," I replied, "That's what they are.
"I've read such since I was a boy."
Then he fixed me with a deepening glare and said,
"Do you know from whence comes what you enjoy?"

"What do you speak of, old one?" I asked
Completely and utterly confused
He then took out a long stemmed pipe, and answered
"Let me give you a clue."
He loaded the pipe's bowl with tobacco from his pouch
And lit it with a wave from his hand
I then with an eerie feeling knew
That he wasn't from these lands

"All these tomes around you," the old man explained
"What you think of as entertainments for your mind.
"Are actually gateways to other worlds
"And other times."
The stranger inhaled the smoke from his pipe
And then slowly he exhaled
And I began to see formed in the smoke
Things of a grandiose scale

Worlds floating before my eyes
Galaxies and stars
Planets and portals in space
So distant and so far
Universes there were, so many more than one
Yea, an infinity
And in each universe, I beheld
A different version of me

I saw myself as a wizard in one
A warrior in another
A God in yet another reality
At war with a rebellious brother
In still another I was a king
And in another, a last survivor of a race
My visitor nodded his head in approval
As he saw amazement dawn on my face

"Yes, there are more realities than just this one."
He said as he continued to smoke
"And they are all wrapped in a beautiful framework
"Of that, I do not joke."
And as he pulled his hood back over his head
His face began to change
And seemed to take on an appearance
Quite fearsome and strange

And I realized to my utmost terror
That his face had become a skull
His teeth locked in an eternal grin
And I began to wail in woe
"You are Death!" I screamed in fright,
"And you have come for me!
"It's meant for me to die this night
"To be taken by such as thee!"

His voice softened as he said
"Do not fear! I do not seek to take your life from you!
"It's just in this lonely world sometimes
"Even Death seeks company too."
I shivered as he laid
His hand of bone on mine
And then I felt a calming magic
Blanketing my spine

"You have entertained an angel unaware
"And for that, you shall receive great reward
"You will live for many happy years
"More than you could hope to afford
"If there were more folk like you
"It would be a far merrier world
"For a light that fills the multiverse shines
"When such kindness is unfurled.

"Fare thee well, Lord of Goyce
"And remember the truth you have seen
"Reality is so much bigger and wondrous
"Than mankind could ever dream."
And with a laugh from his white jaws
He faded from the room
And never will I forget that night
When Death did not come with doom.

INTERLUDE X

It is a very saddening thing to see that all the magic and mysticism of ancient times is seemingly gone from the world. It makes one wonder if, somewhere unseen, the legendary creatures of aeons past are still existing, and lamenting such a catastrophic change.....

THE SAD SLUMBER
OF THE DRAGON

In an ancient cave
So dark and deep
There does
A majestic dragon sleep
His scales as old
As time itself
If into his deep past
You would delve

His mighty wings folded
In the slumber dense
His horned pinions
Their razor defense
But he hasn't stretched
Them in flight for ages
Those times of glory gone
Like faded pages

His hind and foreclaws
Unsharpened and dull
As he has long since
Known a foe
His tail curled about
Resting near his head
The visage that once filled mortals
With dread

Smoke still curls up
Out of his nostrils as he snores
But he doesn't feel the inner fire
As in times of yore
His eyes shut in dreams
Eyes from which tears have fallen
Because he no longer
Hears the calling

Of his brother wyrms
Could he be the last one?
It seems that the
Age of Magic is gone
The world descending
Into dullness and greed
Its shine gone
As it sinks in a materialistic sea

The cancer of harsh rationale
And unbelief
Eating wounds in this sphere
So deep
No one longs or cares
For magic anymore
Minds completely shut off and closed
Not like before

When this great dragon
Ruled the skies
And others like him
In their realms so high
Some friend, some foe
All fierce with power
In their time
In their hour

A time when giants walked
And elves thrived in tree cities
And dwarves would mine deep
For their treasures so pretty
Mermen thrived in dazzling empires
Beneath the sea
And druids would revere
The gods of nature and tree

A time of adventure and peril
Of wonder and might
When the stars would shine
So clearly in the night
And wizards into the
Deepest mysteries would peer
To learn of ancient magicks
That they held so dear

The time of the sword, the lance
And the battleaxe
And the very skies themselves
Would crack
With raging thunder
As angered gods fought their wars
Amongst each other
To prove who was more

And the human folk then
Were nobler it seemed
Filled with honor
And lived by their dreams
Not like today
Where the soul seems sucked out
And the world is in such
Spiritual state of drought

Religion crushing
Such wonders of life
Filling all with fear
Hatred is rife
Technology blasting imagination
To dust
And mankind devolves further
In their base lusts

The old dragon stirs
In his sleep with a groan
And lets out
A pitiful, world-weary moan
And uncomfortably shifts
His gargantuan head
If this is the world now
He would rather be dead

INTERLUDE XI

Every warrior worth his strength faces trying times that torment his soul. What he learns from these battles is not that the Gods hate and curse him and want to torture him, but they are forging him into an entirely new, stronger being.

It is always darkest just before the dawn......

THE MARSHES OF DOOM

On this endless quest
Through horror after horror
And challenge after challenge
I reach a place
Where the sky
Is as depressingly gray
As lead

The dirty clouds hang low
Threatening, ominous
Not a patch of blue
Of the space beyond
Is seen
Nor do sun nor moon
Give their light

I see stretched
Before my eyes
A flat, morose landscape
Of nothing but foul, festering marshes
The green grass
Doesn't even give light or hope
All seems dead, funereal
And dark

The gray, slime-filled waters
That surround me
Are stagnant
And populated with flies
And insects that bite
And sting
And a fell odor
Assails my nostrils

I begin to grow weary
But it is not a natural weariness
It is the black sorcery
That this accursed place
Is pregnant with
I climb down off my steed
To keep myself awake

As I walk my noble warhorse
And he whickers nevously
I notice that all the trees
In this sad swamp
Are leafless and skeletal
Depression and blackness
Grows up with them
Out of the very soil
From which they were birthed

I chant an incantation
To heighten my senses
And keep my mind alert
But I am so weary
I feel fatigue
Tugging at me
Pulling me
Down, down into the grave

And I begin to hear
Sinister, whispering sepulchral voices
Coming up
Out of the fetid waters
Swirling around me
Lulling me
Tempting me

"JOIN US!" they chant
"JOIN US!"
"LAY DOWN WITH US
"HERE, AMONG THE DEAD THINGS
"GIVE UP YOUR QUEST
"IT IS NO USE
"ALL IS LOST
"TAKE YOUR PLACE AMONG THE DEAD!!"

My eyes and body
Begin to grow heavy
I am beset
By utter exhaustion
The inside of my head
Grates with pain
But even in my weariness
I still firmly answer "No..."

"YOUR CAUSE
"MEANS NOTHING!!" the dread voices scoff
"YOUR MORTAL EXISTENCE
"WILL WEAR UPON YOU
"UNTIL YOU ARE UTTERLY SPENT!!
"YOU TIRE ALREADY!
"JOIN US HERE
"BENEATH THE DOOMING WATERS!
"GIVE UP YOUR SOUL...."

The eldritch spell
Still thick upon me
I lethargically
Pull my battleaxe
From its sheath
Upon my back
And weakly ready my shield

"Hear me," I croak
"Whatever.. you darkling things
"May be
"It is the spell
"You... weave on me
"That weakens me so
"I will... not give in!
"I rebuke....you all!"

"IF YOU WILL NOT JOIN US"
The ghostly voices rattle
"THEN YOU WILL BE DESTROYED!!"
And from out
Of the stagnant waters
All around me
Ghoulish forms
Arise

Skeletal warriors
An army of the undead
Their black, corroded armor
Strapped to nothing but bone
Their eye sockets
Cavernous voids
Their mouths frozen forever
In the rictus grin of the grave

They clang their swords
Against their shields
They savagely shake
Their battleaxes, maces,
Warhammers, and spears
Their mouths yawning
In a silent roar of bloodlust

And before me arises
Yet another horror
Shrouded in black and gold
Flowing robes
His face too is a skull
And his eyes blaze
With the red fires
Of hell

On his brow
There rests a cruel-looking
Crown of black iron
And his hands
Are shod in black clawed gauntlets
His breastplate
Shines with fell, hellish
Blood-red runes
Of darksome magicks

He towers over me menacingly
And in his right hand
He holds a bladed staff
With what looks like
The faces of the damned
Carved into its blackened wood

"I AM THE MARSH-LICH!"
His ghastly voice grates
"I AM THE LORD OF THIS SWAMP!
"THESE LANDS OF DOOM ARE MINE!!
"YOU ARE NOTHING!
"AND YOU SHALL BE CUT DOWN!
"YOU HAD YOUR CHANCE
"TO GIVE IN EASILY
"BUT NOW YOU WILL PAY!!"

"I...will not give into you!"
I groggily answer
"Your spell...is nothing but illusion!"
And so I call upon all the Gods of Light
To aid me
To empower me
With all I am
And all I have been born to do
And achieve

My axe clashes
In heated battle
With the blade
Of the Marsh-Lich's staff
Sparks fly
With all my might, though I am weak
I fight him
Dark spell-laden missiles of doom
Fly from his staff

And I deflect them
With my shield
The undead horde
Cheer their master on
In black exultation
And the battle begins
To wear on me

But still I fight on
Despite the horror's
Taunts and curses
Proclaiming absolute supremacy
Over my soul
With one last surge of strength
I pour all my will
To push through
Into my enchanted axe
And seal it with spells of light

With a savage roar
I heft my battleaxe on high
And bring it down
Upon the tyrant's skull
Splitting it in two
Along with his ugly crown
His body falls at my feet
And his diabolical spirit
Is carried away moaning
Upon the wind

Likewise
All of the undead warriors
Collapse and fall
Threatening me no more
And I make my way
Out of that swamp
Of loathsome doom
And nightmare

INTERLUDE XII

Our universe is vast. Teeming with galaxies. And each galaxy holds countless systems, that in turn hold countless worlds. With that reality in mind, how can anyone truly believe that we sail alone upon this cosmic sea of night?

UNIVERSAL PONDERANCES

Sometimes at night
When I look up at the sky
And I see the stars blazing
And comets passing by

I begin to think
I begin to dream
Of just what is out there
And it makes me want to scream

How so many people
Refuse to believe
In life out there among the stars
They can't conceive

Of there being other beings out there
Different from us
Such narrow-mindedness
Fills me with disgust

If the Almighty Master
Intended just one planet and race
It would be, as Carl Sagan put it
"Quite a waste of space."

But let's forget for a while
What those naysayers believe
And instead focus
On what I conceive

When I look up at those stars
Blazing in the night
My mind and imagination
Immediately take flight

To distant spheres
And alien worlds
And before me the secrets of the universe
Seem to unfurl

Unbelievable vistas
In the great black void
Vast ships controlled
By brains of droids

Sprawling empires
Of splendour and power
Beings that, if we beheld them
We earthlings would cower

Galactic federations
Of planets and races
So old and ancient
Their beginnings seem traceless

Mighty cities
Brooding cyclopean towers
Incomprehensible entities
With vast mystical powers

Grim and glorious battles
Century-spanning wars
Advanced, mighty weapons
Mankind has never seen before

Fearsome wormholes
Leading God knows where
Powerful cosmic forces
The thoughts raise my hair

These alien beings
Have visited us before
In ancient ages past
In times of yore

Sumeria, Egypt
Atlantis, Babylon
These ancient kingdoms echo
A vast cosmic song

Aztec, Toltec
Inca, and Mayan
Star-spawned technology
Made them fierce as lions

Hyperborea, Ultima Thule
Lemuria, Atlantis, Mu
These ancient mythical empires
Saw the celestials too

Roswell, New Mexico
Area 51
The Shadow Government interferes
They won't let alone

The cosmic complexities
That mankind deserves to know
They maliciously cover up
What they've found greedily, like crows

But there will come a day
Where they'll no longer lie
The cosmic truth will be presented
Before our very eyes

I look very much forward
To that day
The day of first contact
Where the naysayers will say nay

No longer
And our eyes will be opened
To the fact that we are no longer alone
And we'll pass from this age
To a more enlightened one

That's what I see
When I look up at the stars
Out into the heavens
So impossibly far

INTERLUDE XIII

The Nephilim were on the earth in those days--and also afterward--when the sons of God went to the daughters of humans and had children by them. They were the heroes of old, men of renown. **GENESIS 6:4**

And just where did these terrifying giants of old disappear to, now that they are no longer found upon the Earth? To terrorize other worlds amongst the stars, of course......

ASSAULT ON NAMKAAGH
(An Epic of the Anoghian Paladin Platoon)

Here I sit
Strapped in and waiting
With thirty others
Of my homeworld

I hear the roar
And whine
Of the engines
Through the hull
Of the stolen and refitted
Nephorath Troop Lander
My guts start to curdle

The commander
Stands before us
Giving words of instruction
And encouragement
His helmet
In the crook of his arm

I see his
Triple rows of teeth move
And his jaw-stingers
Curl and uncurl
But I can't seem to hear
What he is saying

My threefold heart
Hammers so hard
That it seems
That I can hear none else

My breath
Whooshes deafeningly
Through my helmet's respirator
And the catch-tube
Pops into my mouth
As my battlesuit reads
That I'm about to vomit

And I do

"Are you alright?"
I hear my friend and compatriot
Zaltak ask at my side
I swallow back
The burning bile
And just nod

I gaze again
At Commander Mynch
Tall and resplendent
In his ornate battlesuit
And flowing cloak

Nothing but the highest
Admiration and respect
Has filled my core
For this individual
And the thought
Of him possibly dying in battle
Grieves my mind
To even consider

I am Nygan
Soldier in the Paladin Platoon
Of the Anoghian Infantry
And our mission
Is a deadly one;
To infiltrate
The Fortress of Namkaagh
On the world of Anok
Where the vicious
Nephorath Empire
Is said to be building
A powerful weapon

These Nephorath fiends
Have been our sworn enemies
Since time out of mind
When the High Cosmic Presence
Itself decreed
That they would be exiled
From a distant planet
Named Iurthe
And they spread
Their poisonous tyranny
To other worlds
Throughout the Great Void
Including Anoghia
Thus has it ever been

The klaxons
Within the ship
Begin to wail
Alerting us
That our landing
Is imminent

"This is it, boss!"
Zaltak hisses at me excitedly
Again, I simply nod
My friend and I
Are fresh from the Academy
This is our first mission
Long have we trained
And I can tell he is excited
While I am a nervous wreck

I feel the harsh thud
Of the ground beneath us
And Commander Mynch
Orders us into formation
As the bay doors open
And the walkway descends

The commander leads us
Into a dense and foreboding jungle
Our force
Spreading out
Into two columns

The two Source Priests
Flank the commander
Their channeling staves
Used as walking sticks
While I, Zaltak, and the heavy infantry
March behind

At our backs trudge
The bladesmen
While the grenadiers
Fall in behind them
And the sharpshooters
Bring up the rear
Taking to the treetops
With their jetpacks

As the jungle swallows us
The bladesmen move to the
Very front to cut down
Any dense or dangerous foliage
That may obstruct our path

All seems eerily quiet
Even the wildlife
Seems silent

As I slowly traverse
The greenery
I feel some unseen thing slither
And wrap itself
Around my leg
And faster than a blaster bolt
I am yanked into the air
And dangled by a slimy green tendril
Over a gigantic ravenous maw
Bursting with razor-sharp teeth

I realize with paralyzing fear
That I am
In the twisted arboreal clutches
Of a sarmoth
A giant, man-eating, semi-sentient plant

I hear my fellow soldiers shouting
Laser beams and projectiles fly
To eradicate the growing abomination
That has chosen me
For its meal
But to no avail
For its outer skin
Is as hard as stone

Only I have the proper position
To take out this menace

As I am dangling
I see its thorn-covered tongue
Begin to raise up toward me
And beneath where its tongue did rest
I see a purple, eye-like orb
I now know where to aim
I unholster my heavy blaster
And squeeze off three shots

As the green-colored blasts
Bathe the inside
Of the creature's mouth
With deadly light
It sounds an ear-shattering squeal
As its inner eye
Is completely obliviated
And its tint turns
From dark green
To a rotten brown
As it breathes its last

Zaltak helps me
To my feet and asks me
If I'm alright
I answer yes
And continue
The slow march

The platoon enters
A steep uphill climb
And suddenly
The sound of plasma repeaters
Fills the air

Commander Mynch roars
To drop to the ground
And a notification within
My helmet's comm system
Prompts me to switch
To a private channel

The commander informs us
That there are two pillboxes
At the top of the hill
Out of which Nephorath soldiers
Are gunning for us

The sharpshooters
In the treetops
Cannot accurately aim
From that vantage point
And anyone without
Explosive projectiles
Is most likely
To be mowed down

And so the grenadiers
Are commanded
To crawl forward
Through the undergrowth
And assault
The pillboxes

Metallic orbs
Of propelled silenced detonators
Sail up from
The jungle floor
And launch themselves
At high speed
Toward the small openings
In the pillboxes

I see the blinding fire
Of the explosion
And hear the agonized screams
Of the Nephorath guards

The grenadiers inform the commander
That all is clear
And as we continue
To make our way uphill
There is no evidence
Of any remaining Nephorath
Just charred and crumbling stone

We come
To the edge of a cliff
A great expanse
Stretches out before us
The bottom hidden by mist
And upon the cliff
On the other side
Of the expanse
Broods the great fortress
Of Namkaagh
In all its grim glory
And covering the space
Is a vast bridge
That of which
Ten men can walk fully abreast

Abruptly behind us
The grinding noise
Of a gatt-blaster rips the air
And four of the grenadiers
Covering us at our flank
Are mowed down
And I turn my head to behold
Six looming Nephorath
Each at least ten feet tall
And the breadth of roughly
Two and a half men
Their helmets come to a wicked
Pointed beak
Above their fang-laden mouths
And the exposed skin
Of their jaws and lips
Is a sickly gray

What appears to be the sergeant
Marches ever forward towards us
Spraying a lethal barrage of projectiles
From his caltrip-pistols

They must have come up
From a bunker under the pillboxes
I think to myself
As Mynch barks orders
And we scramble for cover
Behind a group of boulders

The commander screams into
His comm device
Demanding to know
Where in the multiple hells
Our sharpshooters are
And no sooner are the words
Out of his mouth
Than they emerge at the edge
Of the jungle canopy

As the commander
Squeezes off shots directly
At the enemy sergeant
From his plasma rifle
A lancing blast fires
From the treetops
And hits the hulking Nephorath
Carrying the gatt-blaster
Blazing him in the back
Of the head
And dropping him instantly

The commander finally
Nails the sergeant
In the exposed lower half
Of his face
Ending his relentless advance
For good

Then to my utter horror
I witness one of the
Nephorath guards
Aim a flamethrower
At the treetops
And fire

The entire treeline
Is set aflame in a flash
And I hear screams
From the sharpshooters
As the fire consumes them
And their jetpacks explode

"You son of a grondac bitch!"
I hear Zaltak scream
And I know he must be
Incensed with grief
As one of the sharpshooters
Is his twin brother, Balzac

He relentlessly fires
Angry emerald bolts
From his blaster rifle
And I join in the firefight
Screaming in rage

I manage to hit
The guard's backpack tank unit
And the Nephorath whorespawn
Erupts in an inferno

Lined up in formation
As we are
Behind the boulders
Commander Mynch shouts
For all members
Of the heavy infantry
To open fire
And mop up
The remaining Nephorath

The demon halfbreeds
Stand no chance
As they are cut down
In a hurricane of blaster fire

We cautiously emerge
From our cover
And thank the Divine Source
That no Nephorath
Across the bridge
Guarding the dark fortress
Have heard us
They must have been
All taken out by our sharpshooters

We count our losses
And we are fortunate
All of our force remains
Save for two of our six grenadiers
And our sharpshooters

We are surprised
When two surviving sharpshooters
Rejoin our force
Flying out of the burning jungle
On their jetpacks

One of the two that survived
Is Zaltak's brother
And the twin siblings embrace
With tearful relief

The commander gives us a nod
But warns that our mission
Is not even half complete
And points over the bridge
At the evil citadel's
Cyclopean black towers
Piercing the skies
It gazes down upon us
Like some menacing dark god

I can't help
Feeling a chill in my blood
From staring
At the architectural obscenity
What horrors lay within
I cannot even begin to imagine
Nor do I want to try

Mynch commands
The remaining grenadiers
To detonate the bridge
To prevent any more Nephorath troops
From crossing
And as the charges are laid
He explains that we will scale
Down the face
Of the opposing cliff
And enter the fortress by way
Of the sewage system

He announces he possesses a grapple gun
With a zipline
And that our battlesuits
Will each hook
To said zipline
And carry us across

When the grenadiers
Have fled safely back
From the bridge
A remote detonation
Is executed
The explosion
Is like a titan's roar
Flames consuming
The whole of the bridge
And taking large slabs of it
Down into the cloudy abyss

No Nephorath guards scramble
To the edge
Of the opposing cliff
Either the explosion
Made our enemies deaf
Or our shapshooters
Did one hell of a job
Mopping them up

The commander fires
His grapple gun
And the piton
At the end of the zipline
Punches through
The opposite canyon wall

One by one
We each descend the zipline
Until we are all across
And have activated
The grapple mechanisms
In our armor
So that we are able
To scale the rock

All twenty-two of us
Descend the cliff
Down through the cloud below
And when we have broken through
The thick, white vapor
We see
A giant sewage pipe
Jutting out of the rock

As we descend
To the exit pipe
We notice a grating
At its opening
The framework of which
Prevents anyone from entering

Two bladesmen
Are employed
To use the plasma-field
Around their vibra-swords
To cut their way
Through the grating

Once they have done their work
We enter in formation
Once again
Behind Commander Mynch
And his Source Priests

We have to activate
The floodlights
On our helmets
As all is pitch black
The green sludge
Of the sewer system
Comes up to my shins
I am thankful
For the artificial air
Cycling through my suit

The commander advises
Keeping a sharp eye
Because any nightmare
Could be lurking
In the dark
Beneath the Nephorath fortress

Through seemingly endless tunnels
We travel
No sign of hostiles anywhere
But we discover in time
That we are not alone

I hear an eerie clanking
On the ceiling above us
I look up
And my heart freezes
In terror

Crawling upside-down
On the pipes above
Shamble an army
Of horrific mutant creatures

Below their gaunt torsos
They possess the bodies
Of serpents
Which they use to coil
Around the pipes
To keep them aloft

And from their fingers
Grow long, wicked talons
Their skin is
Bone-white, wet, and scaly

I silently tap Zaltak
On the shoulder
With my trembling finger
And point up towards one
Of the scaling horrors

I hear him breathe in
Sharply through his helmet
And it is then
In that absolutely disquieting second
That the thing moves its head
And stares straight at us
With its bulging eyes

The abomination
Opens its puckering mouth
Impossibly wide
And emits a cacophony
That sounds like a cross between
A deep, throaty roar
And a wet, sucking noise
The fins at either side
Of its flabby neck
Lift and rattle
Threateningly

Out of pure fear
Zaltak fires two shots from his blaster rifle
Missing his target
And is about to fire again
When the thing drops
From the ceiling
And all of its brethren
Drop down upon us

I hear Commander Mynch
Shout to execute
A circle formation

The commander moves himself
Into the center
With his Source Priests
Our two sharpshooters
And three remaining grenadiers
Form the inner circle
While our four bladesmen
Form the second
And we twelve
Heavy infantry units
Form the outer circle

"Blast the bastards!"
The commander barks
And we heavy infantry
Cut into them
With our blaster bolts

Over seventy of the filthy monsters
Are slithering toward us
On all sides
I notice that our shots
Are being deflected
By these beasts
By long twin
Blade-like protuberances
That appear to grow
From their forearms

"What kind of genetic freaks
"Have the Nephorath left
"Down here?!"
Zaltak shouts
Above the blaster fire

I'm about to answer
When I hear
A heavy infantryman
To our left yell
"Aim for their gut, boys!
"Then aim for their heads!
"That will knock 'em down!"

Zaltak and I follow the advice
The filth do not expect us
To burn a hole through
Their guts upon first blast
Leaving them surprised
And vulnerable enough
To have their heads blown off

The infantryman to our right
However
Is not so fortunate
As the slithering monster
Sees its opening
And takes his head
With one swipe
Of its bladed arm

His fellow soldier
Who was right beside him
Screams in anger and grief
Blowing the mutant
In the side of the head
And goes on a rampage
Mowing down three more
Of the sewer-scum
Until his body is sliced
To ribbons
By three who close in on him

I don't believe
I will ever be capable
Of ridding his harrowing screams
From the echoing corridors
Of my mind

The two sharpshooters
Balzac, and his partner, Jyzen
Are felling the scaled slime
With ease
From their perches
In the shadows
Two kills became four
And four became six
And on and on
Until it becomes a competition

Our three grenadiers
Deal absolute destruction
With their deton-launchers
While the Source Priests
Summon up violet bursts of mystic energy
From their channeling staves

The bladesmen are commanded
To the front
At certain intervals
And like savage berserkers
They dispatch the brutes
With their vibra-swords
The arm-blades of the blasphemies
Being hacked off
And proving no match
For their plasma fields

Fiend by slippery fiend
We whittle them down
Until they retreat
Back into the shadows
Back into whatever dark nest
They came from
The primitive rejected experiments
Are hopeless
In the face of
The power and might
Of the Paladin Platoon

With praising words
From our commander
We gather back into marching formation
And journey on

******

Out of the muck
And the mire
Of the sewer systems
We reach the lowest levels
Of the Citadel of Namkaagh

We have turned off
Our floodlights
To avoid being spotted
By the enemy
It is still very dark
Save for a few
Glow globes
Placed in wall sconces
That glow a hellish crimson

According to the fortress schematics
That were given to us
By the Zormphon spies
We are now in the dungeons
And the commander informs us
That we have a mission down here
As well
For one of the spies
Has been captured
And is being held and tortured
Down in these godforsaken depths

As we travel through
The nighted twisting corridors
Even though they are
Still quite high and wide enough
To accomodate the Nephorath giants
I feel the hallways closing in
Like they are going to suffocate
And crush me

I notice saddened, pitiful
And scared faces
Of various interplanetary beings
Staring from behind
The force fields
Of their prison cells
And I feel for them
I quickly speak up
On our private comm channel

"Commander Mynch, sir
"With all due respect
"I think we should let
"These other beings free."

"Negative, Private Nygan."
His voice rasps
"We can't be held responsible
"For their lives
"As well as that
"Of the Zormphon prisoner."

Sergeant Calia
The leader of the heavy infantry
Interjects
"If I may say so, sir
"Private Nygan is right
"We can't leave those prisoners behind
"What's more is
"If they choose to accompany us
"We will have more
"To fight on our side."

There is silence
For the space
Of a few seconds
Then the commander answers
That the sergeant had made
A good point
And orders her
And three of our heavy infantry
And one of our grenadiers
To stay behind
To rescue the prisoners
And then return
Once their task is complete

My friend
Is one of the four
Asked to assist in the rescue
And I am worried
But Sergeant Calia
Assures me
That he will be alright

Our platoon stealthily moves
To the end of the corridor
Where there waits
A large steel door
With a Nehporath guard
To either side

As the giants spot us
The commander shouts
For us heavy infantry
To set our blasters
To silenced mode

Before the hulking demonspawn
Can shout out in alarm
We lance through their armor
And they crumble to the ground

Grabbing a keycard
From the person of a dead guard
Mynch unlocks
The large door
And as it slides open
I and my comrades
Witness a gruesome sight

In a wide
But dark chamber
Lit only by
A few red glow-globes
A Nephorath
Clad in a white, sleeveless
Gore-stained tunic
Bends his obscene bulk
Over a strange, cruel-looking apparatus

In the infernal light
We see other macabre machines
Of torture
Scattered throughout the room
The highest technology
Used for the lowest and most reprobate of means

The grisly monster
Slowly turns toward us
His long hair in ratty knots
A single horn protruding
From the center of his bulbuous forehead
And his eyes glowing
The same color as the globes

"Oim efraid yer too late,"
He laughs
With a voice like a grating
Trash compactor
"This 'un had no information
"So I's done with 'em!"

We see a device behind him
That resembles a sizable metal box
And out of the top of it
We can see the Zomphon's
Sagely head

Oddly enough, its face
Has the look
Of complete tranquility
Its four eyes all shut
As if in deep meditation

The Nephorath torturer
Presses something on the device
And a transparent dome
Closes over
The poor prisoner's head
And explodes it
In a splatter
Of yellow gore

"You overgrown, grey-skinned bastard!"
The commander screams
"All heavy infantry open fire!"

"B..but Commander," I stammer
"Shouldn't he be taken to trial?
"Instead of...a full-on execution
"Right here?"

Mynch grabs me by the gorget
"You heard the order, Private!
"Don't make me smoke you
"For treason!"

My fear at the commander's
Harsh words and manhandling of me
Shifts as I see
The brutish Nephorath
Heft a colossal cleaver-like blade
And raise it high into the air
With a fierce growl

I pull off several shots
And so do my fellow infantrymen
And we scramble
Out of the way
As the immense, charred corpse
Falls smoking to the floor

"Never mess with Paladin Platoon
"You Watcher-spawned filth!"
Commander Mynch spits
As he kicks the dead torturer
In the teeth

If he still is wroth with me
He doesn't say anymore about it
Nor does he have time to
As a large bay door
At the other side of the dungeon
Ascends
And a squad of Nephorath
Bursts in

They are led by a sergeant
Who points at us
With a wicked-looking sword
Commanding his troops to attack

As the gargantuan enemy
Fires into our ranks
The commander snarls
For all to take cover
Behind the various torture machines
Spread throughout the dungeon

As the brilliant colors
Of blaster fire
And launched detons
Criscross over the dark chamber
I take cover
Behind a chair with straps
And some sort
Of huge disk-shaped gun facing it

I observe two
Of our four remaining bladesmen
Leap to attack the sergeant
In the center of the room
With flips, kicks, and pirouettes
They engage and dodge the sergeant's
Savage sword arcs

Then I notice a third bladesman
Drop from the ceiling
Onto the sergeant's shoulders
And thrust his steel
Through the Nephorath's exposed neck
And just for good measure
The fourth bladesman
Runs the behemoth right through the gut
Sending him crashing down

The commander fires his blaster
Like a man possessed
While the Source Priests
Hunkered down with him
Fire lightning bolts
From their fingertips
At the enemy

One of the bladesmen
Is shot through the throat
While trying to get back to cover
While a grenadier's
Head is blown off
By a deton
As he peeks out
From cover

I switch on my commlink
As it suddenly hits me
What I am hiding behind

"Commander!" I exclaim
"I am in the cover
"Of some sort of sonic wave device
"I can see the turret
"In front of me."

"If I can turn
"This sonic weapon
"Up to its highest setting
"And aim it at the Nephorath
"It could prove to our advantage!"

"Brilliant thinking, Private Nygan,"
The commander's pleased voice answers
"Get your ass on that turret
"And cook those overgrown s.o.b.'s now!"

"Yes sir!" I shout
And hop on
The commander meanwhile
Orders our platoon
To activate full audio protection
Within our battlesuits

Another of our heavy infantry units
Falls in a barrage of blaster fire
And a sharpshooter
Picks off the dead one's assailant
As I carefully aim
At the Nephorath
At the far end of the chamber

Locking it in
To its highest setting
And activating my own
Audio protection
I say a quick prayer
To the One That Is All
And I fire

Huge translucent circular waves
Of sonic decimation
Are released from the weapon
And into the enemy force

All of them scream
In excruciating pain
And clap their hands
To the sides of their heads
But it is of no use

Their monstrous forms
Drop like Myrtignian flies
And the chamber seems to quake
Under their collapsing weight

Commander Mynch
Commends me
For my idea's execution
And the rest of the platoon
Enter the torture chamber cautiously
Having returned from their mission
To the prison cells

Thankfully all are intact
Including my friend
And five rescued prisoners
Have now joined our ranks

They all introduce themselves
With salutes to our leader
Tresslas, a bulky Reptoid from Sigma Draconis
Who has sworn off the oppression
Of the dark Reptoid Empire

Nabchula, an acrobatic, yellow-furred being
From the jungle world of Mynga
Who has sworn vengeance on the Nephorath
For conquering her people
And forcing them into slavery

Duul and Dran, twin sorcerers
From the small race known as the Unar
Who also were forced into slavery
By the Reptoid Empire
Who are allies
To the Nephorath

And Zamnozz, from the insectoid race
Of the Chirrans
Being grateful for his rescue
For he was going to be used
In cruel experiments

According to the schematics
The turbo-lift
At the end of the chamber
Led straight up
To the top level
Of the fortress
Where the Nephorath weapon
Was said to reside

All twenty-six of us
File into the turbolift
Which can accomodate
Our numbers easily
As it was designed
For the mammoth Nephorath
But we find, strangely
That it is no longer operating
Perhaps a failsafe
Was built into the camera
That Commander Mynch destroyed
With his blaster
When we entered the lift

At any rate
We decide
To climb through
The maintenance access hatch
In the lift's ceiling
And scale the shaft

We climb the maintenance ladders
On the right and left walls
Of the shaft
All of us
Except for Zamnozz
Who can simply ascend
Using his wings

He agrees to scout
Further upward
To see if there
Are any nasty surprises

It's not long
Before we see
Red fire
Being shot from
The Chirran's pilfered blaster rifle
And we hear
His buzzing voice
Warn us
Before a storm of sickly white wings
Surround him
And rip him to shreds

"By the Source!"
I exclaim to Zaltak
Bringing up the rear below me
"What are those things?!"

"Strag!"
He curses under his breath
"Those creatures are Grykim!
"Very nasty!"

I had heard
Of the Grykim before
They are said to be an interplanetary scourge
Able to transform the makeup
Of their bodies
So they can travel through
Deep space
And birth their spawn
On myriad worlds

Their nests were usually found
In cavens deep underground
And in dark places
A turbolift shaft
Was a perfect place
For them to thrive

Before I realize it
I hear a sickening squeal
Directly above me
And the dreadful wings
Of one of the beasts
Descend on me
And I am grabbed
By its sharp talons
And whisked into the air

Looking up at the thing
That has me in its clutches
By the illumination
Of my helmet's light
I see its clusters of night-black eyes
Gazing down at me
With malicious intent
And its dog-like muzzle
Draws back to reveal its carnivorous teeth
Its wicked tongue
Darting across them
In a display
Of vicious bloodlust
As it soars me back
To its nest

I recognize that obviously
Although these vermin
Are dwellers of the dark
They are not sensitive to light
One less potential weapon
In our arsenal against them

I also realize
That I am so far up the shaft now
That if somehow I manage
To kill this nightmare
I'll fall to my death

If I could only get it
To veer
A little closer
To the nearest service ladder

I unsheath
My vibra-knife
And ram its blade
Into the Grykim's leg

The winged horror
Voices a grunting scream
And a fierce hiss of anger
As the pain
Makes it swerve
Toward the ladder
I was aiming for

Meanwhile, I see the brilliant colors
Of blaster bolts
And laser beams
Lighting up the dark
As more of the fiends
Swoop down
In a plague of wings

I witness both monster and soldier
Fall to their death
I know not how many
For my mind is focused
On battling my current adversary

The horrible freak
Voraciously tries to bite me
With its demonic fangs
I barely dodge its attack
And hit the activation switch
On my vibra-knife
Embedded in its leg

The blade
Cuts itself clean through
And the devil's leg falls into the chasm below
As does my knife
And I soon find myself falling
As if in slow motion
Black blood from the creature's
Severed limb
Dripping onto my faceplate as I plummet
And the horror flapping away
Now disinterested and in searing pain

As I know I am plunging
To my doom
I quickly mouth a prayer
That my journey to be united
With the Supreme Cosmic Being
Will be an easy one

I feel something grab me
Around my torso
And attach itself
To the nearby ladder

I find I am staring upside-down
Into the simian face
Of Nabchula
As I hang from her prehensile tail

"You are lucky, Anoghian,"
She smiles wickedly,
"That we Myngans can see
"So well in the dark
"And that we are so acrobatic
"I believe you owe me one."

"I'll buy you a Tyraxian ale
"Once we're offworld," I answer, out of breath

"Done," she smirks
And sets me right-side up
Putting me on the rung below her
And no sooner am I placed back down
Than I observe
Her swiftly unsheath
Her recovered vibra-sword
From her back
Holding it poised in her tail
Activating its plasma field
As the Grykim
Plunges back down
For the kill
Ferocious maw wide open
And claws lusting to tear flesh

With an ear-shattering warcry
Nabchula swings the glowing blade
And severs the blasphemy's hideous head
Letting it plummet with the rest of it
Following after

The Myngan can't see my expression
Behind my faceplate
But she knows I am astonished
And gives me a sly wink

Not three seconds later
The both of us are captivated
By a net of bright cerulean energy
Closing around three more Grykim
And sending them hissing and screaming
To their dark graves

The commander's voice
Pipes up on the comm system
"Alright, men
"Looks like we've cleaned up
"The Grykim trash
"Thankfully, the Source Priests
"And the sorcerer brothers
"Thwarted that last attack
"With a combined spell."

"We've suffered some losses
"But we must press on
"Just another stretch of climbing
"And we'll reach the top chamber
"Keep your wits and senses sharp!"

As I continue to climb behind Nabchula
I look across and my floodlamp
Illumines the fierce-looking Reptoid
Who gives me a quick, approving nod
The two, child-sized Unar sorcerers
Are strapped securely to his back
I consider the beautiful irony
That the universe manifests

******

We all emerge
From a crawlspace
And enter a monstrous, cavernous chamber
The vaulted ceiling is so high
It is lost in shadow
The entire room is one large dome

My platoon has lost even more
Of its members
The commander and Source Priests remain
But only five of the heavy infantry
Have survived
Three bladesmen are with us
Along with two grenadiers
And two sharpshooters
And of course, the four rescued prisoners

Nineteen of us remain
And I wonder what that number
Will be cut down to
When this mission ends

"Looks like this is it,"
My friend says to me
And I am thankful
That he is still alive
Along with his brother

"Whatever happens," he says firmly
Planting his gauntleted hand on my shoulder
"It's been great fighting alongside you."

I try my best
To choke back the tears
"Likewise, my friend," I whisper.

Commander Mynch orders us
To all fan out behind him
And to be wary
For this is the last stage
Of our mission
And this weapon
Whatever it is
Should be within this chamber

"Welcome," a mocking, booming voice sounds
And from out of the shadows
Steps an exceptionally tall Nephorath
Dressed in elaborate black and crimson robes
With a triad of horns
Growing out of his head
With his wicked, pointed, short beard
He resembles a grotesque hybrid
Of goat and man

"Lord Ruulgh.."
The commander spits out
The fiend's name
As if it is poison
On his tongue

Ruulgh mockingly bows
Gripping his staff
Which seems to be cast into the form
Of a fell, monstrous worm
"A pleasure to make your acquaintance, Commander."

"The pleasure's all yours, scum!"
Mynch barks
"I don't play nice
"With a sick zaprash like yourself
"That pals around with demons!"

"Oh, that's a shame,"
The towering Nehporath sighs in mock sadness
"Because all of you
"Are about to be an integral part
"Of this operation."

An honor guard of twenty Nephorath troops
Come out of the darkness behind Ruulgh
Leveling their blasters at us
While a hatch in the floor
Opens behind them
And a giant mechanical archway
Decorated with sinister-looking runes
Rises into place

"You've heard about our new weapon, I trust,"
Ruulgh smirks noxiously down on us
"But it's not a weapon in the sense
"Of a blaster or plasma beam
"Or disruptor
"Or any such object
"You see, this weapon can change time."

"The means to travel through time..."
I blurt out loud in awe
"Your empire has acquired it?!"

"Indeed, my brave Anoghian friend,"
He sneers
"The Emperor's aim is to use it
"To travel back to when Enoch, your ancestor
"Worked with Yahveh against our fathers, the Watchers
"And had them bound in the prison of Tartarus
"We will kill your meddlesome progenitor
"Before he even begins communication
"With that tyrannical fool, Yahveh!
"When we succeed
"You Anoghians will have never existed
"And our Spirit-Lord, Satanus
"Will have complete sovereignty over Earth
"And the entire universe!
"Hail to Emperor Ogus
"Who has brought forth
"This master plan!"

"Hail Emperor Ogus!"
The enemy troops shout
With fanatical zeal

"You...you speak blasphemy!"
My comrade Zaltak rages
"You can't defeat Yahveh!
"You don't stand a chance!"

"Oh, trust me," the foul Nephorath Lord chortles
"The Emperor possesses more than enough ambition
"To try
"And you fortunate ones
"Are going to be the first
"To enter the time-gate
"We shall strip you
"Of your armor and weapons
"And see how the primitive
"Peoples of Earth react to you!"

Lord Ruulgh punches
A quick configuration
Into the strange archway's console
And a blazing, swirling
Blue field of energy
Pulses within
The gateway is open

"You're not getting away with this!"
Howls Nabchula over the roaring din
Of the time portal
"Not if I have anything to say about it!"

Like lightning, the Myngan leaps
Through the air
Artfully dodging the blaster fire
Flying at her
And while the Nephorath
Are distracted with her
We take our opportuninty
To open fire

Standing atop the portal
Directly above the machine's
Green-glowing crystal
Nabchula unsheathes
Her vibra-sword with
Her tail
And screams
"This is for my people!!"
And plunges the blade, plasma field activated
Into the crystal
Her fingers squeezing off shots
At our foes
With her twin blasters
At the same time

The portal overloads
With crimson lightning
That cruelly courses
Through the body
Of the Myngan warrior
And the interdimensional gateway
Changes from blue to blinding white

Time seems to slow to a crawl
As a being
With a face that shines
Like a thousand neutron stars
In brilliant flowing white robes
Steps through the device
And catches the charred Myngan
In his arms
As she falls

From behind the stranger
Two towering Seraphim
Who dwarf even the Nehporath
Enter through the time-door
Irradiant in immaculate white armor
Encrusted with precious stones
Their majestic wings
Covered with eyes that see all

With one flash
From each of the angels'
Flaming greatswords
Every last Nephorath trooper
Is decimated

Gently laying the charred corpse
Of Nabchula down at his feet
The shining visitor
Speaks with a voice
Like thunder
"Your time here is at an end, Ruulgh!"

The Nephorath necromancer
Shielding his face
From the interloper's light
Snarls with venom,
"Who are you?!"

The light from the creature's face dims
And all of we Anoghians
Fall on our faces
When we realize
Who stands before us

"You!"
Ruulgh hisses
"Enoch, the meddlesome one!
"Who has always held the favor
"Of Yahveh!"

The two titanic Seraphim
Move to strike
The haughty Nephorath Lord down
But Enoch shakes his maned head
And they snap back at attention

The ancient one
Unsheathes a staff
From his back
And holds it before him
Its headpiece
Decorated with
The connected orbs
Of the holy Sephiroth

"You will accompany me
"To be placed in the prison of Tartarus
"With your demonic fathers,"
He firmly proclaims

"You are power-drunk, old-man!"
Ruulgh spits
"I will not go without a fight!"
He levels his worm-staff at Enoch
And channels forth
Night-black lightning
But before his spell can reach
The old one
Our age-old father holds his staff on high
And surrounds himself
With a blinding white orb
Absorbing the dark magic blast
And dissipating it
Into nothingness

He hurls the orb
From himself
And into Lord Ruulgh
Shattering the villain's staff of power
And knocking him with a resounding quake
To the floor
His robes lie in tatters upon him

"Nephilim Lord, your power is shattered!"
Enoch exclaims
"And in the Name of the Most High of the Cosmos
"I bind you with a threefold cord!"

Ropes of searing golden energy
Lash out from Enoch's staff
Wrapping themselves around
The necromancer's mouth, arms, and wrists
Suspending him in captivity
In midair

"Rise, my children, rise,"
Our father says with a smile
Upon his bearded lips
"Blessed refugees, rise as well
"You have no reason to bow before me."

"We know greatness
"When we see it, my lord."
The Reptoid Tresslas grates
As he stands

"And I know greatness
"When I, in turn, see it,"
Enoch laughs
"You are brave warriors
"All of you
"Especially you, my children
"You mighty Anoghians
"I know your Queen Mother
"Who now rests with me
"In the Beyond
"Is proud of you."

Tears fill my eyes
As I remember
Our beloved Queen Tralia
Who fell in love with our Father
Aeons ago
And birthed our race

The silence is broken abruptly
By the whine of ships' engines
Echoing through the chamber walls
I smile at Zaltak
As Enoch says his goodbyes
Taking Ruulgh with him as his prisoner
And restoring Nabchula to us
Back from the dead
With a final approving nod
He, the broken Ruulgh, and the Seraphim
Exit through the glowing portal
And are no more

I can tell by the sound of the ships' engines
That the Anoghian interdiction fleet
Has arrived right on time
We are going home!

INTERLUDE XIV

Blessed is he who opens a book, for therein before him doth lie a gateway of the highest of magics.......

TOMES OF HIGH ADVENTURE

Upon my hand-crafted wooden shelves
In a room so blissfully peaceful
Yet crackling with unseen energy
There are assembled strange and wonderful objects

These objects, although they may look humble
With their bindings of leather, paper, cloth, and wood
They hold a power within them
That cannot be fathomed in its awesomeness

For they are portals
Portals to the myriad dimensions
That are scattered throughout
The very multiverse

The words that flow
Upon the pages within
Hold a magic
Of unbelievable power

Where one can be transported
From a dull and lifeless world
To one full of wonder, enchantment
Danger, and adventure

Truly, I have experienced many adventures
Through these objects
That are called "books"
These tomes of wonder

I have travelled with two hobbits
On a quest to rid the world
Of an accursed magic ring
Of terrible power

I have quested for three lost mystical swords
Forged by an ancient and strange race
To stop an undead horror
From threatening the world once more

I have crawled through dark dungeons
Teeming with indescribable horrors
Alongside a barbarian
Of fierce might and adventurous spirit

I have wandered the terrifying gulfs
And voids between the worlds
Where dark alien vistas that blast the soul
And terrible Elder Gods reside

I've seen vast interplanetary wars fought
With lasers lancing blindingly
Out of hulking battle cruisers
And swift starfighters

I have done all this and more
I have lived a hundred lifetimes in one
Which, without the aid of these mystical tomes
I would not have been able to do

True adventure awaits
Between the covers
And in the pages
Sprinkled with the printed word

INTERLUDE XV

It is the belief of this writer that we can each create our own reality, and banish the demons tormenting us to a tartarian prison from whence they can never return. Every one of us has that power within us, for we each possess the spark of the Divine....

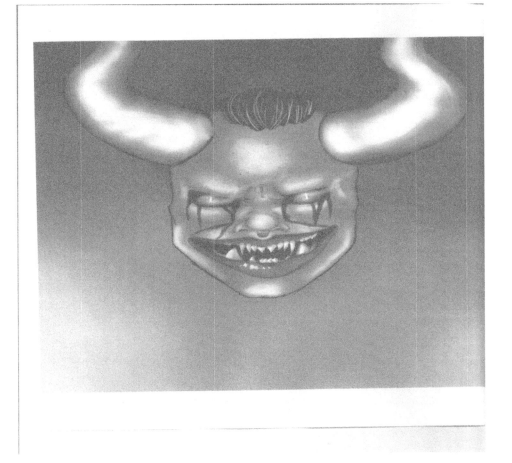

GREAT CYCLOPEAN SHIFTS
IN THE EVER-FLOWING CONTINUUM
OF REALITY

I once thought I stood upon solid ground
I had convinced myself
My reality was completely molded and shaped
When it came to one particular issue
In my mind's eye
I had forged in the hallowed smithy of my inner consciousness
The particular part of the realm I now stood upon

The crimson colours of heat in the cosmic forge had
Seared themselves upon my vision
I heard the clank of the hammer upon the anvil
The hiss and bubbling of cooling water
I and the inner servants of my mind and heart
In this great forge sang Songs of Earth and Power
Of Water and Wind
Of Ice and Mountains
Of Stone and of Fire
Of great gladness and inspiration
Of awe and reverence
Of pride and satisfaction
Of grief and the sharpest, most agonizing of pain
And of anger and resentment

Yes, in the molding of this new reality
That I so desired, I poured in all of my being
All that I was, am, and will be
But something about it didn't seem quite right
When the gleaming, finished product emerged

Oh, it was beautiful and filled with wonder
And throbbed with positive cosmic energy
But something about this reality, this modification
To the world I had created for myself
Seemed to have this wrongness about it
And it worried me
But yet I let it go

Now I see this reality crumbling about me
Its flaw became its killing stroke
Mountains crumble and the earth shatters
The seas heave and begin to boil
Volcanoes erupt and molten lava spews forth
The sky turns black and blood-red lightning
Rakes the dying landscape

And out of the deepest pit
I begin to hear cruel, maniacal laughter
The demoniacal colours of Chaos
Sear themselves upon my mind
As my Old Enemy rises from the abyss, larger than a mountain
Its hideous features distorted by a triumphant grin
Its cruel minions and underlords surround it
In a fury of batlike wings, horns, tentacles, hooves,
Myriad eyes, fangs, claws, beaks, manged fur, scales, shadow
And black fire

From its cavernous maw comes its black mocking speech
"THINE OWN WORLD, YEA, THY VERY REALITY
"HAS TURNED ITSELF UPON THEE
"NOW SURELY I WILL USE THIS AS MINE OWN WEAPON
"AGAINST THEE, AND REVEL IN THY TORMENT
"DARKNESS HAS FALLEN, AND NOW IT IS TIME
"FOR ME TO TAKE UP MY BLACK REIGN IN FULL
"FOR ALL ETERNITY!"

With tears in my eyes and pain in my heart
I answer the fiend
"No! My whole reality did not crumble
"Just a part of it; a fraction
"I will not let a piece of hell-spawned filth
"Such as yourself revel in this small fall I have taken
"I will not let you establish your black throne
"Over my mind once more!
"I now gladly accept the dying of this realm
"As one small step in the great cosmic quest
"You shall not gain one ounce of victory from it
"I shall return to my forge, to rebuild
"And imprison you in the pit of shadows once more!"

I draw my ensorcelled blade and begin to chant
Runes of Light surround me
My enemy writhes in agony
With a scream that shakes the very multiverse
I plunge my steel deep into its eye
And then withdraw it
With swelling pride and militant spirit
I wipe the black ichor from its gleaming surface
I hold out my hand
And with my full belief
Chant the spell that imprisons
The Black Foe back into the Abyss

I fly into the very center of the swirling
Storm-wrought clouds
And thrust my sword aloft
 "Now," I intone, "If this realm must die
 "Let it be done! And let me embrace it
 "So that I can build for myself a new reality!"

All that exists before me
Is sucked into the very tip of my blade
And I awaken in darkness
Not an evil darkness
But a comforting one that surrounds me
Like a blanket
And I see the fires of my great forge
Begin to glow once again......

INTERLUDE XVI:
FRAGMENTS FROM THE CHRONICLES
OF KING LAGMOOR

On March 22nd of the year 2124 A.D., the planet Earth sent out a robotic exploration force to Jupiter's frigid moon of Europa, hoping to find evidence of past extraterrestrial life. When the droid explorers cracked the icy surface of the moon and descended into the ancient oceans beneath, they found more than they could have ever dreamed of.

For far in the freezing watery depths was discovered a perfectly-preserved metropolis of awesome architecture and breathtaking beauty. All inhabitants of this majestic city were long gone, not a corpse to be found. But the decorations, statues and motifs of the elegant and magnificent sunken abodes seemed to tell the tale of a society ruled over by a matriarchy, more specifically a lone warrior-female.

More answers came when they found a pocket of air within what appeared to be the grand palace, and found a breathtakingly preserved library. Here were found the fragments from the Chronicles of King Lagmoor, a king who had reigned before the coming of the warrior queen depicted in frescoes and statues about the city. Within these fragments was found a prophecy by Lagmoor about the coming of this queen, and her union with him and the dispelling of the darkness that existed on this world.

No one knows just how old this place is in galactic history, or just what cataclysm happened here but more data is being gathered presently and will be released as more significant findings are revealed...

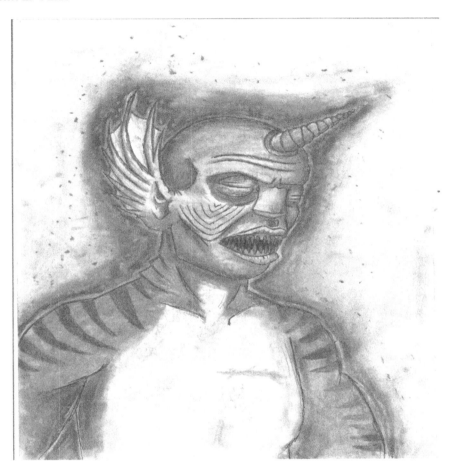

THE TEMPLE
OF
KRRASSATH

Across the black sands of the Desert of Woe
Under two blood-red moons
In a land that forever embraces the night
Like a passionate lover
Lies a city where even Gods dare to tread

In the great nighted city of Sskraal
Great black basalt towers
Raise their obscene pinnacles
Becrested with jade serpents to the stars

In this dark, cyclopean metropolis dwell the Sskorrm
An ancient and terrible race
Of serpent-like, reptilian beings

Over them rule the six Serpent Lords
Terrible to behold
Dwelling in their blasphemously enormous Palace of Venom
Upon their jade thrones
That glow with an eldritch green light
But it is not the Serpent Lords
That truly rule this city or this land

In a gargantuan temple
Of black obsidian
That dwarfs the size of the palace
And dominates the skyline of this sinister city
Through cavernous corridors decorated
With foul hieroglyphs of this hideous race's dark past
In an immense chamber
Before a great, blood-stained black altar
Lies a perfectly rounded, immensely wide
And mind-bogglingly deep pit
Encircling this pit
Are fell, blood-red runes
Carved into the black, mirror-like floor

It is here that the Sskorrm gather
To worship their terrible dark god, Krrassath
Otherwise known as the Treacherous One

In this vast room
The Clerics of Venom assemble
In their voluminous black robes
Perfoming unspeakable rites
To please their putrid god
And their dark deity is quite
Terrifying and maddening to behold

Out of its black pit
Which leads to only the Gods know where
The Foul One rises to devour the firstborn
Of every female

It possesses the body of a giant serpent
Whose numerous scales are pure obsidian
And from its scaly neck rear two human heads
One male, the other female

From its maws beladen with razor-sharp fangs
And disgusting, forked tongues
It speaks with a voice
That would drive a mortal insane
If they were to hear it

And far below the temple
In chambers black as midnight
Shamble the undead corpses of souls
Eternally condemned to no rest
By the black shamans of the Sskorrm

These are the remains
Of the heroic, noble peoples
Who once ruled this land and dwelled in this city
Before the Great Darkness came
And they were conquered by the Sskorrm

Now this wicked city
Flourishes in eternal night
And the Treacherous One
In its lair of subterranean blackness
Laughs

FRAGMENT I:
LUST FOR WAR

Alone I sit in my darkened hall
Upon a throne of sorrow
Wondering deep within my soul
Will there be a new tomorrow?

Demons haunt me day and night
Black things of chaos torment my soul
I long so much deep within my heart
For the One who will make me whole

She was foretold in ancient prophecy
By the Keepers of the Flame
That when dark times came unto my land
She would stand by my name

She would hail far from the Lands of Light
And wield great power within her hands
She would mass a great army of Valkyries
And rid the foulness from the land

I too, am a warrior
My axe is never dulled
My great hall is decorated
With my enemies' screaming skulls

But the dark powers proved for me too great
And ravaged my whole realm
I feel I have no will to fight
To don my once-proud helm

I've been tormented and beaten and dragged through the mud
My heart has been torn in two
My mind has been ravaged, my soul has been raped
I feel there is nothing I can do

Outside my shattered fortress, werewolves howl
Ravens eat the dead
The triumphant war songs of once-proud men
Have turned into songs of dread

The light that once was in me
Now is no more
It is conquered by the dark
Yet there remains in the bowels of my soul
A little glimmer, a spark

And it tells that too long have I sat in the shadows
Too long have I waned old
Too long has it been
Since I've seen the age of glory and gold

I warn you now, Son of Hell
Betrayer of the Light
I will do everything within my power
To end your eternal night

My sword longs to taste your blood
My axe hungers for your head
My broken but determined heart of war
Lusts for the day you are dead

If I should die before your demise
Then I gladly accept my fate
But my battlecry will carry on
To put an end to your reign of hate

Oh mighty Gods of War
Be with me now
Imbue my steel with might
Fill me with the lust for the kill
Prepare me for the final fight

I pledge to you my life, my soul
Now let vengeance fill my sword
I wish for no gold or jewels or riches
The Blasphemer's death shall be my reward

FRAGMENT II:
ECHOES FROM MY BROODING THRONE

Loneliness is a black disease
An all-consuming worm
It fills the soul with sadness
Its sickness a foul germ

For what seems like millenia, I've battled it
I've been nailed to a black cross
I've cried tears of the deepest sorrow
And felt heart-breaking loss

Every day I ride into battle
Bloodlust in my eyes
My warrior soul longs to hear
The Black Foe's defeated cries

Loneliness is but one of the weapons
In the Dark God's arsenal
That tears out the heart of the heroic
And devastates the soul

It seems an eternal battle between
This black force and I
Many Gods of Light has he slain
In my ears I hear their dead cries

Ensorcelled though my armor is
With mighty spells of Light
I am greatly troubled
When I face the Demon God of Night

The rapturous joy of battle
When I make his black hordes cry
Seems to be overshadowed by fright
When I see his hellspawned eyes

Yet I must continue in this war
Against my enemy sworn
And I eagerly await the day
When I shall be borne

On the wings of a golden griffin
Her sword gleaming in the twin suns,
The Goddess shall come through the Gate of Seven Moons
And my enemies shall run

And together with her Valkyries of Vengeance
We will decimate the foe
And then, after a millennia of suffering
My empire shall be made whole

FRAGMENT III:
THE MOCKING HORROR

When I was a younger ruler
And my realm still was grand
And it had not been conquered
By the Demon God Ocdagoroth's fell hand

There was still a threat to my people
A shadow in the East;
A wicked, power-hungry emperor
That would consume my realm like a beast

It would eventually be that I would crush this despot
With military might and magic at my command
But on the Eve of the Sabbath of Guorm
I embarked on a journey into his lands

On a mission of peace
To negotiate a truce
So that I might bring my kingdom
Out of his noose

Forty knights I took with me
And my lead sorcerer Draalek
Seeking their protection and company
In this long, hard trek

The whole journey
I need not chronicle here
But there is one happening
Of which I wish you to hear

In the foreboding, ragged Mountains of Ryath
Under the bleak twin moons by whose light we camped
Came a soul-shattering scream
That prompted us to light our lamps

We explored the area with great fear
Anxious of what we would find
I started in surprise
When my sorcerer tapped me from behind

"Look!" he commanded
Magic light pouring from his staff
And I saw the frightening source of the sound
That now let out a mix of scream and laugh

It stood nearly fifteen feet tall
From head to toe, it had fur with mottled spots
On top of its shoulders it had two hyena heads
And from its fanged mouths came the smell of rot

The eyes of the monster glowed an eldritch green
Its claws sharper than steel
And in its beastly, titanic hands
A club of iron it did wield

The hideous laugh-scream came again
From both mouths it issued forth
I stolidly urged every man of my company
To stand firm for all they were worth

Proud on the outside, but shaking within
I strode to face the beast
"State why you disturb our sleep!" I commanded
"Before I take you piece by foul piece!"

"We are the Trarl, guardian of this pass,"
Said the left head, and then began the right
"What a pathetic force
"You have gathered here this night!"

"We never asked for your approval, demon!"
Said my sorcerer, eyes flaring with rage
"We seek an accord with a ruthless tyrant
"The Emperor Tirage"

"We know of him," bellowed the left head
"But to reach his palace
"Us first you must pass
"Tell us why we should let you through
"You worthless sons of an ass!

"Your men are so pathetic
"So ugly and small
"If we were as pitiful as you
"We wouldn't have a will to live at all!"

"Gaze upon us!" the second head commanded
"For we are perfect and strong!
"We have the features of the Gods!
"That after which you long!

"You are not like us, you filthy worms
"So we must stamp out your life!
"We'll make it quick and painless
"If against us you don't strive."

"Foul werebeast abomination!" I scoffed
Drawing my sword from its sheath
"When I sever your two filth-ridden tongues,
"No more boasts will come through your teeth!

"For I am the mighty thane of the bright realm of Bralach
"Of the heroic line of the Thagars
"You will rue this night you challenged me
"And my men of war!"

"Then come forth, O brave and mighty king!"
The hellish creature mocked
"We'll make you wish you never set foot
"On our beloved rock!"

I then sounded my battle cry
And all my knights drew arms
And my sorcerer set to work
Summoning spells and charms

And thus my mighty men did charge
With me directly at the head
The monster too charged and slammed its iron club
And instantly one-fourth of them were dead

Amazed dreadfully at the sudden loss
I heard the behemoth brag
"You see, you cannot beat us!
"We will turn you all to bloody rags!"

Then suddenly Draalek
Leveled his staff with a great shout
And from it, blasting straight at the beast
A beam of blue fire shot out

It broke its club to splinters
And knocked the demon to the ground
But unbelievably, it rose right back up
And emitted again that awful sound

Of insane, screaming laughter
And at the sorcerer it sneered
"Puny, pathetic mage!
"Is that all you can do here?!

"If you think our cudgel is our only weapon
"You've made a vast mistake!
"For we hold a power within us
"That will make you maggots quake!"

Then the demon's twin heads sucked in air
As if to devour the world
And out of its mouths came a horrible blast
Made of green fire, round and curled

When it hit my knights at the very back of the line
They fell upon their knees
Banging their heads upon the ground
Sounding heartbreaking pleas

As I was recovering from the shock of the attack
The fiend suddenly made another
And the middle of my force went straight to their knees
Every knight with his brother

I turned unto my sorcerer and gasped
"What foul magic is this?!"
But he was lost in thought, meditating
As if in some far abyss

Like a volcano, my anger rose
My eyes so full of tears I couldn't see
The berserker ways of my ancestors
Now called out to me

I didn't care if I lived now
Or if I became one of the dead
All I wanted was to take
This foul beast's two heads

Like lightning, the monster's blast hit me
And I fell upon the ground
Now everywhere I looked
There was darkness all around

I seemed to be floating
In some negative void of space
And I felt this black feeling come upon me
That made me feel so base

It told me I was a pathetic king
To just give up the fight
To accept that my day is done
And to embrace the dark night

My body was wracked with immense pain
I screamed and cried great sobs
I crawled on my belly like a worm
And began to curse the Gods

Then I heard a voice call out to me
As if from far, far away
"Great King, your men lie broken in the demon's spell
"It is up to us to win the day!"

"Draalek, is that you?" I sobbed
"Yes my lord, it is I
"I have retreated from the great fiend, carrying you
"And have found a place to hide

"But not for long, for I hear its footsteps
"And its blasphemous laugh
"You must arise out of that black place
"Before it breaks us all in half!"

"I cannot!" I screamed in agony
"I am nothing, I'm a worm!
"This monster is right, it'll crush us all
"And under its heel, we'll squirm!"

"Gods of Hell!" Draalek cursed
"I command you to come out!
"Great King, arise out of that hellish place
"Speak the words now! Shout!"

"Words? What words?! I have no words!
"Of which to shout or say!
"What words are these that you speak of?
"Tell me, great wizard, I pray!"

"Why, the words my Order blessed your ancestors with
"Three hundred years ago
"An incantation of protection for your kingdom
"For it to prosper and grow

"Hear my voice, come back to the Light
"Now repeat after me
"*'Torghak Samar Orgklinach!'*
"And repeat it times three!"

With every fiber of my being
I invoked the spell
And in doing so, pulled myself
Out of that dark hell

"I have discovered," said Draalek
"A way to kill this beast
"I should have thought of it before
"But it didn't occur to me in the least

"Your shield," he pointed, "You know it's magic."
I slowly answered, "Yes."
"And also you know the great deflection power
"With which it has been blessed?"

The realization hit me like a warhammer
Why hadn't I seen it before?
Now I surely had a way
In which I could settle the score!

I marched forth proudly, and faced the fiend
And challenged, "Do your worst!"
And from the two heads came the sick laughter-scream
And then the devastating burst

With quicksilver speed I raised my shield
And deflected the attack
And from my enchanted shield toward the monster
It deflected back

The sorcerous blast hit the creature
And hurled it to the ground
And from its two heads issued forth
A pitiful whining sound

I climbed upon the hell-thing's chest
And jeered at the beast
"How does it feel now to know
"You are the very least?!"

Then with a terrible scream
I hacked off both its heads
And used them to decorate my hall
With my other trophies of slain dead

The spell was broken on the knights still alive
They awoke as if from deep sleep
And from there we made our way
To the Mad Emperor's keep

But as I said, I shall not chronicle that here
My purpose was to recount
The black-spawned thing we faced that night
On that terrible mount

FRAGMENT IV:
A PAINFUL MEMORY

There was a time I should have forgotten
Long, long ago
To this day, when I think back
It still rips and tears at my soul

To the far southeast of my kingdom
Lay the land of Tarassos
A hot, arid desert land in the day
And in the night, it all but froze

I, my chief wizard, Draalek
And a retinue of my honor guard
Were on our way to this desert land
On a mission of peace, not of the sword

We were headed for the capital of Saroph
Of the mighty monolith stones
Where the great Queen Haphatiri
Ruled from her golden throne

Haphatiri was one of my strongest allies
A comrade I was glad to have
And we were en route to her kingdom
To discuss matters of trade

We crossed the Akysos Desert
On the great winged Erekaphs
And finally we reached the great city of Saroph
In all its magnificent mass

I marvelled at the solid gold pyramids
The jewel-encrusted temples of splendour
The magnificent cyclopean towers
And all the beauty this metropolis rendered

Then I turned to my chief wizard
His face was downcast and brooding
"What ails you, my old friend?" I asked
Trying not to sound too intruding

"I sense a great evil here," he answered
With fear and foreboding in his eyes
"Here lies, I feel, a monstrous malevolence
"Against which my very soul cries."

"Rest assured, Draalek, I'll keep an eye out."
I said with cool assurance in my voice
"But perhaps it's only nerves that trouble you
"You didn't have to come, it was your choice."

And with a dark look, he shook his head
And simply said no more
I began to feel concerned for him
But that was right before

I saw the great palace rising into the clouds
A truly awe-inspiring display
And all concern I had in my mind
Simply melted away

And then I saw her descending the great steps
A true vision of beauty indeed
I had never looked upon Haphatiri before
Now within my loins stirred with a deep need

Her skin, it seemed
Was golden like the sun
And her hair, black as the night
To her buttocks it did run

She wore a headdress of solid gold
And eyeshadow that brought out the blue
She was beyond beautiful
This was certainly true

She wore a brief gold breastplate
Riddled with precious stones
An immaculate loincloth draped down from her hips
And her legs were left bare alone

Two servants trailed behind her
Their heads completely shaved
Their countenances were stoic
Neither joyful nor grave

"I welcome you, King Lagmoor,"
The beautiful queen said
She offered her hand and I kissed it
And gently inclined my head

"As you know, Great Queen," I answered
"I have come on a mission of peace
"It is my greatest hope that Tarassos will be our ally
"And that our friendship would never cease."

"A noble cause, to be sure," she smiled
"We will talk, come enter in
"I must say that your wizard, though
"Looks like he's run afoul of gin."

I put my arm around Draalek
And joked, "Buck up, old friend
"Surely this is the most unlikely place
"For you to meet a grisly end."

"Heed my warning," he said gravely
"I feel the threat here is true
"I worry not for myself
"I worry solely for you."

"What could there be to worry about?!" I laughed
"For this is paradise!"
But I would later find out
How wrongly I surmised

That evening was absolutely lovely
The stars were shining bright
And I looked down from the palace balcony
At the glorious city bathed in moonlight

It was then that Haphatiri came to me
In a revealing evening robe
And my heart began hammering
As if to burst out of my chest, it strove

She said, "Your men are all cozy in their apartments
"And now it's just you and I
"I must say I find you irresistable
"Though to hide my feelings, I do try

"I have been praying to the Sand Gods for a lover
"And I believe you are the answer to my prayers
"Do you feel the same way about me
"When into my eyes you stare?"

"Yes," was all I said
And I embraced her with ultimate passion
And kissed her with an all-consuming desire
That elicited the same reaction

We made love upon the balcony
Beneath the shining stars
And I experienced passion that night
That took us inexplicably far

I awoke the next morning
In my wizard's apartments upon his bed
And a great pain there was
Pounding in my head

I started to rise
But my wizard gently forced me back
"Rest easy, my king," he said
"You've suffered quite an attack."

"What happened?" I asked groggily
I was quite confused
And Draalek began to give me
Some quite disturbing news

"I saw you with the queen last night
"Upon the balcony
"It was very perilous, and had I not acted
"There would have been tragedy."

"You did what?!" I growled in anger
"You were spying on me?!
"Why would you, my old friend, do this?!
"Is this betrayal I see?!"

"Nay, my lord, not betrayal!
"I was most concerned for you
"I have seen evidence of that which I felt
"And I see it's true!"

"Damn you and your superstitions!" I roared
"How dare you spy on me!
"How dare you go behind my back
"And breach my privacy!"

"You know yourself," the wizard answered
"What you say is truly a lie
"You believe in the ways of the Gods
"Just as much as I

"Listen, for when the queen kissed you
"She planted upon you a spell
"And from her lips came a poison
"That drips of liquid hell

"Luckily, I have cured the poison
"It would have made you a mindless drone
"But I see her spell is still upon you
"And it chills me to the bone!"

"You're lying!" I sneered
But Draalek forcefully said, "Wait!"
"I have something to show you
"That will further warn you against your fate."

Then he placed his hand atop my head
And the whole room fell away
And lo, I saw a scene
That filled me with dismay

Deep within her palace
Dressed in night-black robes
The queen stood before a black altar
Behind which an idol towered with malignance full

The towering idol which I saw
Was also obsidian black
And from its eyes glowed such a maleficence
Of which evil did not lack

It was the effigy of Krrassath
Dark Serpent God of the Sskorrm
Who are an evil, black-hearted reptilian race
And more vile than trasag worms

Around the obsidian altar there were
Other black-robed acolytes
And chained to the altar there was
A naked slave girl, shivering with fright

"Oh Great Serpent God of Power!" the queen intoned
As the acolytes chanted strange words
"We give to you a sacrifice
"To appease your hunger of blood from the sword

"And I henceforth ask you
"To give unto me great power!
"For I swear by the blood of this virgin slave
"That this is the Warrior King's final hour!"

She then brought down a wicked dagger
Off which the torchlight streamed
And the vision came to an end
With a soul-chilling, bloody scream

When I finally came to
I tore from the bed in frustration
And I shouted at my wizard in anger,
"Lies! All lies and fabrications!"

"But my lord!" he implored with a hurt look
"Silence, Draalek!" I fumed
And with aching heart and aching head
I retired to my rooms

In anger, I lay down to take a nap
And when I awoke
I was shackled to a vertical table
And a raspy voice behind me spoke

"Well, sso thiss iss the great Warrior King
"Of fabled legend and lore
"The very ssight of you
"Makess my sstomach ssick and ssore!"

"Who are you?" I asked the voice
It was then that he came around
And I nearly burst from the table
To which I was securely bound

The being was cloaked in black robes
Just like my wizard's vision showed me
And when I saw the visage of this figure
I saw the truth of what he told me

Shadowed by the hood of his robe
The creature had the head of a snake
And yellow, hideous glowing eyes
That made my insides quake

His skin was a scaly, sickly green
His mouth bristled with fangs
And out of his maw flicked a forked tongue
Off of which some slime did hang

"And I know of you, you slime!" I spat
"Your race is a blight on this world!
"Foul serpentine filth!
"You'd make a dragon's nostrils curl!"

With a mocking bow, the fiend hissed,
"You give me far too much credit
"I am but an emissssary
"But I am flattered that you dread it."

"A Sskorrm with a saucy mouth," I quipped
"That's nothing new, you piece of dung
"If I weren't held down by these shackles
"I'd rip out your forked tongue!"

"But that can't be done, my darling."
I heard a dusky voice say
And there she stood before me
I felt so horribly betrayed

"Why?" I asked, "Why did you do this?"
With tears running down my face
And then down my cheek
Her fingernails did trace

"Poor, poor Lagmoor," she laughed
"You're such a pitiful fool
"I did it to simply bring about
"An expansion of my rule

"The Sskorrm Empire has promised me
"Legions of the undead
"To use as my troops to conquer the world
"And to take my oppressors' heads."

"And your end of the bargain?"
I asked, my heart breaking
The emissary hissed,
"Ssimply that your life will be ourss for the taking."

"Why me?" I asked
"What will you gain from that?"
The Sskorrm's glowing eyes
Gazed hungrily upon me like a cat's

"You have immensse power within you," he rasped
"You are the fabled Warrior King
"Think of how much power your removed heart
"To uss would bring!"

"You're mad!" I spat
"And how do you suppose to remove my heart?
"Surely your barbaric race is devoid
"Of such a precise art."

Then he showed me his hand
Brandished with some complex, wicked glove
"Our race," he gloated evily,
"Posssesssessss technology you couldn't even dream of!"

Just then the dungeon doors
Completely blew apart
And into the chamber flew
A huge, fiery dart

The ball of fire incinerated the emissary
In the twinkling of an eye
And Queen Haphatiri vanished inexplicably
With a heartrending cry

And in the doorway stood Draalek
Looking positively drained from the spell
He told me that my troops had eliminated Haphatiri's cult
And now all was well

Years have gone by
And the Kingdom of Tarassos is revived
Under a new benevolent ruler
Haphatiri's brother, it survived

And as for the Sskorrm, well
They're still out there somewhere
And the very thought of those serpentine demons
Raises my every hair

And where Haphatiri mysteriously vanished to
Not even my chief wizard knows
It might forever remain a mystery
As to where exactly she did go

And tonight, as I gaze at the stars
I still think of her
And part of me tells me to forget her
That she was just a loathsome cur

And then there's the other part of me
That just can't let her go
My brain warns me against it
But my heart fights back with a no

Either way, I'll always remember
That magical night under the stars
Where our passions burned so brightly
That night has left a scar

FRAGMENT V:
CRIES OF THE LOST CHILDREN

Somewhere in the Ghariost Mountains
Beneath the gaze of an eerie moon
I came to a mist-shrouded graveyard
Where a presence whispered of doom

I led my horse between headstones
Searching for a place to camp
The earth squelched beneath its hooves
Disgustingly muddy and damp

Though moonlight illumined my path
The darkness here seemed to thrive
Pregnant with malignancy
As if it were almost alive

Without warning, I heard a ghostly moan
And then I heard another
In no time at all there was a chorus of moans
Emitted from these ghastly brothers

I drew my blade and shouted, "Who's threre!!"
My steed began to shake
I patted his neck and cooed to him
Calming him for both our sakes

I proceeded, my blade before me
Demanding again who was there
But of any physical manifestation
I saw neither hide nor hair

The moans began to grow louder
So loud they pierced my brain
I decided I must do something
Before they drove me insane

I then remembered the sacred ritual
Of calling on the dead and unseen
Indeed it would be risky
I had to keep my senses keen

I proceeded to draw forth my palm
And sliced it upon my blade
And sprinkled the blood upon the grass
That was as green as jade

I poured my blood to form the sign
Of the Pentacle of Truth
And in around the sign, I carved the names
Found upon the Divine Demon's tooth

"I command you, spirit, to show yourself!"
I chanted the sacred call
"You are compelled by the power of the Seventh God
"To reveal yourself, your all!

"In this circle of summoning, you shall remain!
"You will not step out to harm!
"You only shall be free to return to your plane
"When I conclude this charm!"

The sacred sign I produced began to glow
A searing bloody red
And from the blackness, I saw appear
A true vision of dread

From the sigil below, to the sky above
Swam a host of disheartening shapes
And when I discerned just what they were
It made my whole soul quake

They appeared to be dead infants
All emanating a sickly yellow tint
And parts of their bodies, mostly their heads
Were torn and horribly rent

And from the holes and grisly wounds
Flowed out their rotten guts
These were no simple scratches
Or merely shallow cuts

Some of them did not have eyes
Some did not have mouths
Some were simply torn-off heads
That grotesquely floated about

Suspended in utter terror
I heard them begin to speak
They spoke in eerie unison
And my soul grew weak

"Oh mighty and brave warrior king
"Forgive us for disturbing you so
"You have come to this place as an innocent
"You mean us no harm, we know

"But please, we beg you! Listen now!
"Hearken and hear our tale
"We see in you a pure heart
"That for our cause would not fail!"

And I answered, "Truly, you dishearten me!
"From where and whence do you come?
"You poor, forgotten Children of the Grave
"Oh so far from home."

"Our mothers were taken from the continent of Nhasor
"By a dark and evil cult
"And we, their children, were disposed of
"Faster than a lightning bolt!"

"By the Sacred Gods!" I gasped
"Who would commit such an act?!
"I have seen many atrocities in my time
"But none like this harrowing fact!"

"In the wicked city of Khruxax," they cried
"Where the fires of industry blaze
"And gothic black towers pierce the sky
"Above the murky black haze

"There resides a cult called 'The Mouth of Gharorg'
"And their dark god demands
"For slaves to be made of all the women of the world
"And their unborn children to die by his hand

"We are those victims, ripped from our mothers
"Taken and robbed of our life
"Our bodies burned in the fires of their god's mouth
"Where evil is so rife

"We must show you for you to comprehend
"The true horror of our plight."
And then and there, they filled my eyes
With many horrible sights

I beheld strange men clad in robes
That were immaculately white
And over their mouths were strange metal masks
That shone frighteningly bright

For hands they possessed wicked, weapon-like tools
All claws and blades and hooks
And the things they did with those thrice-damned things
Oh....I couldn't bear to look!

But I had to! I had to! Sweet Ajarkhas, I had to!
To understand their pain
But the horrors I saw, I shall not repeat
To any soul, not even my kin

When the vision was done, I fell and gasped
"Now I understand!
"Gods of Hell! How you must have suffered
"At those blasphemous hands!

"I recall the spell, and I beg of you
"Fill me with your righteous rage!
"I may be one solitary
"Single warrior-mage

"But I swear to you, Lost Children
"That when the time arrives
"These sick, demented bastards shall pay!
"They shall pay with their very lives!"

I then held up my enchanted blade
And flashes of lightning came
Emanating straight from the ghostly infants
And bathing my body with mystic flame

The flames dissipated
And I felt forged anew
And the moisture in my eyes
I assure you, was not from nature's dew

"Blessed are you, mighty king," they said
"We knew we could count on you
"And we know that when the time arrives
"You'll strike loyally and true."

"Rest assured, dear spirits, I will," I answered
As they began to fade
I bowed to them and turned around
And to my horse I bade,

"Come, Trogar, my old friend
"This is no place to camp
"I have earned too much respect for these dead
"And besides it is too damp."

I calmed my horse
For it was understandably shaking from the sight
And I climbed up high into the saddle
And rode into the night

FRAGMENT VI:
THE MENACE IN THE NORTH

She came to me
In a dream
And pleaded for my aid
She was Jyscana
The Priestess of the Seven Eyes
Mystical advisor to
King Rosjark of Nogrund
A kingdom far to the North

With sadness in her blue eyes
She revealed
That the king was in
Dire peril
That he had dabbled too deep
Into dark magics
Out of curiosity
And awoken something truly terrible

Being a loyal ally of mine
As he was
I knew I had to assist Rosjark
And save him from the doom
That had now come upon him
When I informed my
Chief wizard, Draalek
His expression turned most grave

"Beware, oh great king,"
He warned
"For what you go to face
"Is an evil most monstrous!"
"What is this evil
"Of which you speak,
"My old friend?" I asked

With haunted eyes, he answered,
"Ages ago, in the North
"Before the Great Cataclysm
"And the shifting of the poles
"There reigned a great empire of darkness
"Drenched with the blackest of magics
"And had traffick with
"The foulest of demons

"Somewhere, far below the ice
"In that frozen tundra of
"The Kingdom of Nogrund
"Lie the dread relics
"Of that dark empire
"And I fear that King Rosjark
"Has summoned an ancient evil
"That has long slumbered

"For this mission, my king
"With your leave
"I must take my fellow wizards,
"Randar and Pesgan
"For I fear my arts
"May not be powerful enough
"If this evil is what I fear."

And so it was
That I traveled with
My three most powerful wizards
And a retinue of my mightiest knights
And set out upon my quest
After we had crossed the perilous passes
In the Slagdar Mountains
Where the fierce blizzard winds blew
Like the breath of a dark god
We came to the frozen Lake Viron
Which we would have to cross
To enter Nogrund

With great care
We crossed the frozen waters
Praying to the Gods
That they would not crack
Beneath our weight
We had made it near half-way
Across the lake
A chorus of angry howls
Surrounded us
Inhuman, grisly shrieks
That chilled us to the bone

Through the falling snow
We began to make out
Just what made
Those frightful noises
Towering above us
At the height of five grown men
Were monstrous beings
Covered in shaggy white fur

Their eyes glowed
As blue as coldfire
Up from their lower lips
Protruded razor-sharp fangs
And wicked barbed tusks
Emerged from their cheeks
In their mostrous hands
They brandished iron-shod warclubs

Jalbek, the captain
Of my retinue of knights
Rode up beside me
On his steed
As he whispered;
"Ice giants, my king!
"Fearsome, beastly, foul creatures!"

"Indeed, Jalbek," I answered,
Shivering from more than the cold
"We must break through these brutes
"To get across the lake."
"Don't worry, my lord," Jalbek growled
"The Wolf-Brothers shall defend you!"

There was a heavy booming
Of monstrous feet across the ice
And a inhuman scream of rage
As one of the ice giants
Rushed our force

With a berserker rage
Borne from a thousand hells
Jalbek charged the monster alone
His steed snorting as it galloped
Jalbek raised his blade on high
But was thrown through the air
As the fell giant
Decimated his horse
With one heavy sweep of its club

"Jalbek!" I cried, "Do not be a fool!"
The leader of the Wolf-Brothers
Seemed to lay deathly still
As the furred beast
Stomped toward him
And raised its war-club
To deliver the final blow

Then from where my chief wizard stood
I saw a purple-coloured blast of magic energy
Fly forward
And hit the giant
Right between its glowing eyes
And stunned it
So that it fell unconscious
Upon its back
The boom of the impact
Shaking the frozen lake

It was then that Jalbek rose
His wolf-helm glinting
And his black cape billowing
In the wintery wind
And with another rage-filled cry
Plunged his sword
Into the fell thing's heart
The monster gave a scream of agony
And then it died

As the captain was walking back, steedless
Towards his knights
I turned on Draalek in anger,
"You fool! With the fall of that giant
"The ice could have broke
"And killed us all!"

The younger, blond-haired wizard, Pesgan
Answered me cooly,
"My king, it was I that fired
"The stunning spell
"I knew that the ice
"Was thick enough
"From the way the giant
"Rushed across it."

"Very well, Pesgan," I relented.
"But know this, my lord,"
The younger wizard warned
"Those iron clubs
"That those bastards carry
"Are strong enough
"To break the ice to bits!"

There were still six
Of the gargantuan devils remaining
And with their shrill howls
They all raised their war-clubs
"Teeth of the Divine Demon!" I cursed
As their clubs fell
The ice shook once more
Beneath us

Great cracks began to form
And tore the frozen lake asunder
Many men and horses fell
Into those icy waters
Screaming for their lives
The ice had broken up
Into various chunks and islets
Of which my men were trying to gain purchase

For many, it was too late
Half my retinue of knights
Were taken down
Into the icy depths with their steeds
Never to surface again
I was one of those who fell
Beginning to sink
Into bone-freezing oblivion

How long I was down there
I know not
But a hand reached down
And pulled me back up
Onto a sizeable islet of ice
Where my three wizards
And fifteen of my knights still stood
Including Jalbek
They were all that remained
Of our company

Across the rift of the freezing waters
We saw the Ice Giants howling in rage
Shaking their cudgels in the air
Incensed that we had survived
And out from the six behemoths
There appeared a seventh
One that we hadn't seen before

Its beard was braided and plaited with human bones
And a girdle of human skin covered
Its beastly loins
Belted by human skulls
Skulls also it wore as a necklace
And it carried a crude, heavy staff

"What is that creature?" I asked in fearful awe,
"It appears to be their shaman,"
Answered Draalek
"They seek to loose their magics
"Upon us now."

As my chief wizard was explaining
A shaft of lightning shot forth
From the ice giant shaman's staff
And incinerated one of my knights
On the spot

"Strong magics indeed
"They have with them,"
Draalek continued,
"Randar, set up a barrier,
"We must have shielding."

The raven-haired wizard
In question nodded in obedience
His drooping mustache
Sagging further
As he frowned with concentration
And began to chant strong incantations
At the end of which
He struck the butt of his staff
Upon the ground
And there sounded
A deep thrum of energy

The beastly shaman sent another
Bolt of magic lightning
At our small iceberg
But this time
A wall of purple energy met it
And dissolved it
Into the magical shield

The shaman howled in frustration
The rest of the ice giants
Echoing his anger and howling
At the skies
While they shook their cudgels
With great wrathful vigor

The remaining knights
Murmurred amongst themselves
While I somberly stated
"It is a shame I did not
"Bring archers with us.
"They would do greatly
"In this situation."

"Have no fear, my king,"
The head-wizard answered
And commanded the other wizard, Pesgan
To put all his concentration
Into reinforcing Randar's magic shield
As Randar worked his arts
The shield glowed in radiance
And stayed in place

Draalek stretched out his hand
Before the shield
And in the center of it
There appeared a red circle
With red mystic runes
Circling about it

With one single harsh-spoken
Word of Power
Draalek inserted his staff
Into the red circle
And a mystic blast
As red as blood
Shot forth from the shield
And consumed the ice giant shaman
Reducing him to ashes
On the biting wintery wind

And so it was
That the cyclopean fiends
Upon seeing the great display
Of the power of my three wizards
Were filled with fear
And ran for their barbaric lives

******

As we came to the fortress of Krogan
The palace of the mighty King Rosjark
We beheld a grim, cold horror
The gates were open
And the guards and sentries therein
Were completely frozen
In a sheen of blackened ice

Each body
Was a rigid corpse
Frozen in time
Covered
In an ebon, icy shroud

"This is a most dangerous situation,
"My king," Draalek whispered to me
"Judging from what has happened here
"The evil that I feared
"Has been confirmed
"I suggest you
"And your remaining knights
"Prepare yourselves
"As I am so doing
"With my fellow wizards."

Wrapping my fur cloak
Tighter around me
From the now darkly supernatural cold
I led the way into the silent fortress
Halls that were once merry
And full of life
When I had visited my friend here
In the past
Were lifeless, freezing, and silent
As the grave

When we entered
Into the throne room
A scene of distress
And black horror
Greeted my eyes
For there
Held fast to the chamber walls
By blackened ice
Was both King Rosjark
And Priestess Jyscana

The Northern King had his head
Hung low with defeat
His mighty beard
Now seeming to droop
Priestess Jyscana looked up
And her green eyes brightened

"My liege!" she said excitedly to Rosjark
"Awaken! King Lagmoor has come
"As I knew he would!
"We are saved!"
"Nay, Priestess..." the King of Nogrund
Somberly answered her
"The evil that has imprisoned us
"Is too powerful, I fear."

With brazen courage
I spoke up
"Come now, old friend
"Tell me that you are not
"Giving up that easily
"You who have been fierce in battle
"And powerful
"Both in mind and body..."

A mocking laughter interrupted me
From the king's throne
Seated high atop its dais
There upon the throne
Sat a figure robed all in black
And beneath his black robes
Was night-black armor
His face was completely skeletal
Like one of the living dead
And his eyes blazed an icy blue

"So," he cackled, "This powerful warrior-king
"I have heard so much about
"Now comes to confront me
"And save his precious ally!
"How heart-warming!"

I gazed upon his pointed rotting teeth
Set in their mocking sneer
"Warmth is certainly not
"What you have provided
"For this place
"Fell thing!"
I answered and drew my enchanted blade
"Identify yourself, worm!"

"I must commend you
"On your astute observation,"
The hideous, armored, corpselike thing leered
"This king you see
"Bound before you
"Dabbled too deep
"Into forbidden magics
"And opened gateways
"Into dark domains
"And so brought me forth
"I am Ghasharnaruz
"Ancient High Emperor
"Of the fabled wicked Empire
"Of Nasghun"

"You see, my king,"
Draalek whispered in my ear
"Everything I sensed
"Was true
"The terror of Ancient Nasghun
"Has returned
"And seeks to fulfill itself
"Through its revived Emperor!"

"I was imprisoned
"For aeons
"By the magics
"Of the meddling 'hero,' Malak,"
Ghasharnaruz continued,
"But now I am free!
"Malak's chains couldn't hold me
"Your upstart wizard there
"Is a descendant of his
"And I shall thoroughly enjoy
"Crushing him
"As well as you
"And your whole pitiful band!"

With a primal scream
Of battlelust
I ran up the stairs
Of the dais
And swung my ensorcelled blade
At the lich's obsidian oblong-crowned head
In a flash
He swept up
His serpent-headed staff
And blocked my assault

Locked in a fierce combat stance
Our two weapons forcing themselves
One against the other
The undead tyrant's staff
Glowing a dark purple
While my sword blazed
A fiery red
We both bared our teeth
At one another savagely

The power of that devil's staff
Became instantly too much
For me to bear
And sent me flying
Over the dais
And crashing to the floor
Where my sword
Was knocked from my hand
And became stuck to the floor
In a sheen of black ice
With a frozen blast
From the villain's staff

"You see, my weak friend,"
Ghasharnaruz cackled as he descended the steps,
"I may have thrived
"In much warmer climes
"In my time before the cataclysm
"But now I have bonded
"With the cold of this place
"And have made it
"All the more oppressive!"

He punctuated his boasts
With another icy blast
From his ensorcelled staff
Which I quickly rolled from
And dodged
Just in time

I began to unstrap my battleaxe
From my back
When I heard Draalek
Shout for me to move aside
I quickly obeyed his warning
And witnessed my three wizards
Summon an armored knight upon a horse
It bore a curved blade in his left hand
And both horse and rider
Were composed entirely of flames

The fiery rider
Charged the lich
And slashed at the foul being's head
With its flaming scimitar
Ghasharnaruz ducked
But his high crown
Was knocked from his head
And completely immolated
By the flames of the sword

As the burning phantom
Turned to circle back around
The darksome fiend
Aimed his staff
To fire off
A devastating icy sorcerous blast
It was then that my retinue of knights
Descended upon him with their lances
While the three wizards chanted
To keep their summoning
Stable on this plane

But even with the necromancer's back turned
He knew the knights were charging
And to my immense horror
And theirs
Four enormous, slime-covered tentacles
Emerged from his back
And entrapped all fifteen knights
Within their clutches
The wizards lost their concentration
In utter shock at this new horror
And their summoning faded from existence

"I am all-powerful!"
The lich laughed maniacally
"Did you truly think
"You would catch me off guard?!"
And as he began to turn around
To face me,
My knights writhing in the grasp
Of his multiple tentacles
I said a silent prayer to all my Gods
And pleaded with the now-imprisoned
King and priestess, that, whatever power
They might have left in them
They would bring to my aid

I heard my wizards began to chant once more
And I felt myself empowered and almost aglow
With a supernatural light
Time seemed to slow incredibly
And I knew that my prayers were heard
I chanted a spell over my magic battleaxe
And with nothing but pure faith in my heart
I rushed and brought down my weapon
At full-force
Upon the fiend's serpent staff
And shattered it in two

His power fully broken
Ghasharnaruz's tentacles withered
And my knights, having broken free
Drew all fifteen of their blades upon
The fell being
The defeated necromancer
Fell on his face before me
Begging me to spare his life

"You are nothing but a coward!"
I spat as I hefted my axe
Preparing to deal the killing blow
When my chief wizard urgently stopped me
"No, my lord!" he boomed as he ran to me
"You are a noble and merciful king.
"You do not want to stain that repute
"On such a worm.
"Let us, your wizards, deal with him
"And send him back to the imprisonment
"From whence he came
"Besides, death would be too good for him!

"As he said, I am the descendant
"Of the ancient hero Malak
"That imprisoned him to begin with
"I hold the right and the power within me."
With a grim nod, I acquiesed
And so it was that my three wizards
Chanted with powerful incantations
Ones that were frightful to my ears
And they sent the beaten fiend
Screaming into a black portal
Never to be seen again

After I and Draalek worked together
To free King Rossjark and Priestess Jyscana
And the king's entire court
We were rewarded with a great feast
And I left with him Pesgan
My third most powerful wizard
To help guide him
In the use of the right magics
And caution him against
The foul sorceries that summoned up
The black horror we encountered

And so it was, that Draalek, Randar
My knights, and myself
Returned to my kingdom
Wondering what other strange, otherworldly adventures
Awaited us.......

AFTERWORD

So have you seen the majesty of the eternal multiverse, and you have seen but a tiny glimpse, an infinitesimal fragment of that great reality that sears the brain to comprehend. Go forth now, knowing in your heart that there is so much more out there than what we mere mortals can perceive......

ABOUT THE AUTHOR:

J.W. Wright lives in the small town of Arthur, Illinois, in a cozy apartment with his girlfriend and fellow writer, Ariana R. Cherry. They both run a small publishing company entitled *Cherry House Press*. With them reside their two lovable yet mischievious felines, Findlay and Sweetie. They both possess an extensive library of books collected over the years, the writers that is, not the cats.

J.W.'s official webpages are found at https://jwwrightauthor.wordpress.com and at https://www.facebook.com/JWWright83

The official website for Cherry House Press can be found at https://cherryhousepress.wordpress.com

ABOUT THE ILLUSTRATOR:

Janae M. Hopper was born in Central Illinois and still lives there on a fourth-generation farmstead with her family. She began carrying drawing tablets around at the age of five years old and hasn't stopped since. She is especially drawn to FX and horror art. This is her second publication, her first being J.W. Wright's first collection, *Bestial Transformation and Other Horrors,* but she hopes to be featured in the future as aname rolling in the credits on the movie screen under the heading, "Special Effects." Watch for here there.

ALSO AVAILABLE BY THIS AUTHOR FROM
CHERRY HOUSE PRESS:

Bestial Transformation and Other Horrors*

Fyre's The Three Ghosts+

*=Available in both Amazon Kindle and print formats
+=Available for Amazon Kindle only

Made in the USA
Las Vegas, NV
25 January 2022